NURSE AT LARGE

'You're dependable and comfortable, that's what counts here.' Dr Hal Dickinson believed that was the only reason he had invited Rosie Simpson to work in his country clinic. So what was this good-looking, vital, dynamic doctor doing falling in love with his new nurse practitioner?

Holly North was born in Cambridge in 1955. She read History at Durham University and in 1978 married her American husband, Sam. His career has taken them all over the world, from New York and Paris to Saudi Arabia and, at the moment, Japan. Holly teaches English and restores oriental carpets when she can—and when she can't, she keeps herself sane by writing about her home country. She's a passionate advocate of the NHS, which looks all the more impressive from abroad, and consults her brother-in-law, who is a paediatrician, for much of the medical detail in her books.

Holly North has written two other Doctor Nurse Romances, *A Surgeon Surrenders* and *Sister Slater's Secret*.

NURSE AT LARGE

BY

HOLLY NORTH

MILLS & BOON LIMITED
15–16 BROOK'S MEWS
LONDON W1A 1DR

*First published in Great Britain 1986
by Mills & Boon Limited*

© Holly North 1986

*Australian copyright 1986
Philippine copyright 1986*

ISBN 0 263 75595 9

Set in 11 on 11½ pt Linotron Times
03–1286–48,500

*Photoset by Rowland Phototypesetting Limited
Bury St Edmunds, Suffolk
Made and printed in Great Britain by
William Collins Sons & Co Ltd, Glasgow*

CHAPTER ONE

'PEEP, peep, peep . . .'

Rosie stirred from her doze and reached out for her watch, which she had placed on the table in front of her. She shut off the alarm after a moment's fiddling and, disorientated, stared around the dimly-lit room, yawning. The magazine she had been reading when she'd dozed off slid to the floor, making a thump that seemed to echo around the silent house, but in his bed Mr Dickinson didn't stir.

Rosie looked at her watch. Two o'clock. Time to check his medication and turn him, she thought unenthusiastically, too comfortable in the depths of the soft armchair to want to get up and do some work. But she was a conscientious nurse and duty called. She eased herself up and went over to see to her patient.

Mr Dickinson must once have been a handsome man, with a strong, aquiline profile and a broad sweep of forehead. Now, however, pitifully thin and in the ravages of his wasting illness, he was almost skeletal, and Rosie had no problem in gently turning him, staightening the sheets and checking his very faint vital signs. He was deeply sedated and gave no more than a hollow sigh as she moved him. It would not be very long now, she knew instinctively. Not that she'd worked a great deal with terminally ill patients — she had spent the last few years on a female surgical ward at Highstead

Hospital in London—but all good nurses had a sixth sense about their patients. Bending over the elderly man in the dim light from her reading lamp, she smoothed his hair back from his face and checked his pupils. Then she marked on the chart that he had been turned and her observations. There was no need for more morphia at the moment; he was comfortable.

Taking care not to make more noise than was necessary, she slipped out of the room and across the landing to the bathroom to wash her hands. She didn't want to wake up the Sutherlands, who were enjoying an uninterrupted night's rest in their room at the far end of the landing. Mr Sutherland's loud snores could be heard even from here, and Rosie suppressed a giggle. How on earth poor Mrs Sutherland could sleep through that racket was a mystery to her! Fancy falling in love with a man, marrying him—and then finding out that he snored as loudly as that . . . The idea cheered her a little. At the grand age of twenty-six and without an offer of marriage to her name, Rosie had come to the conclusion that a settled life with a man had not been written into her destiny. She was a comfortable, capable person, but not the sort that men of her own age seemed to find attractive. She was the sort of girl that elderly male patients adored—big, bonny and cheerful. But marriage to a man old enough to be her grandfather was not a prospect that appealed! The occasional realisation, as now, with Mr Sutherland's loud snores, that marriage was not necessarily a bed of roses, made her feel better.

It was time for a snack, she decided, returning to the comfortable room that the Sutherlands had prepared for her. Since coming down to Devon from London she'd had three night jobs, and not one of them had been as comfortable as this one. At Jacobs Farm they'd been a bit dismayed when they had discovered that she would need heat and light throughout the night, and they'd complained about the cost. But Mrs Sutherland had brought up an armchair from the sitting-room, and a fan-heater to boost the central heating, and a huge vacuum jug of coffee too, to make the night more bearable.

Rosie poured herself a cup of the coffee now and added milk and sugar that had been thoughtfully set out on a tray. She fished in her bag for one of the several snacks she had brought with her to see her through the long night hours and found a Scotch egg and two doughnuts, which she began to tuck into with enjoyment. The problem with working at night was that it mucked up your metabolism. Anyone who'd never had to work all night seemed to imagine that it was possible to survive on the odd cup of coffee and a few biscuits, but they didn't realise that at around this hour there came the terrible craving for lunch. And then, about break-fast time, a sensation that a proper dinner of meat and two vegetables would go down nicely.

'I need the energy,' Rosie would explain as she packed her bag each evening in her parents' kitchen, her mother watching critically as the chocolate and pork pie were put away.

'But it's not as if you're missing out on your other meals,' Mrs Simpson would protest mildly. 'You have a big breakfast when you get back in the morning and a late lunch when you get up at four. You have a proper dinner before you go out to work too! Surely you don't really need all that extra food?'

'I'm working all night, you know, up and down, turning Mr Dickinson.' That was Rosie's excuse, but it didn't seem to wash.

She wiped her greasy fingers on a tissue and reached for a doughnut, pausing only to turn the page of the magazine she had been reading when she had dozed off an hour ago. She'd been in the middle of a rather good story about a woman who had married a Greek millionaire, only to find that his idea of what he wanted from a wife did not agree with hers, and now, finding the spot she must have dropped off over, Rosie began to devour doughnut and story avidly. But her eyelids were already beginning to droop as she reached for her second doughnut, and she had only taken one bite of it before she fell into a light slumber again.

'Who are you? What do you think you're doing here?'

'Mmm?' Shielding her eyes from the brilliance of her swivel reading lamp, which seemed to have been turned directly on her, Rosie woke with a start and a panicky flash of uncertainty about where she was. The Sutherlands', of course. But if she was at the Sutherlands', what was happening? Half-blinded by the glare of the lamp, she could only dimly make out a looming figure standing over her. With an automatic gesture, she went to push back her wavy brown hair from her brow—and discovered that she was still holding the remains of a jam doughnut in one hand. Swiftly she put it on the table and wiped her sticky fingers down the front of her white overall.

'I must have dropped off for a moment.' It sounded a pitiful excuse, but then, why should she have to excuse herself to this stranger? And what was he doing in the house at this time of the morning?

'You haven't told me what you're doing here,' he stated flatly. He had a voice that would have been pleasant to listen to at any other time; educated but not affected, slightly throaty.

'Before I tell you anything, perhaps you would care to explain what *you're* doing, walking around a strange house and disturbing my patient,' Rosie replied hotly. 'And please move that lamp—I can't see a thing.' Reaching out to move it herself, her fingers, still sticky, contacted his. They brushed for perhaps a second before she withdrew her hand as if stung. And yet in that time she had felt the cool smoothness of his skin and the slight roughness of the hair that sprinkled the backs of his hands, and it was like an electric shock, a sensual experience quite unlike anything she had known before. Perhaps he felt something too, or saw her look of confusion, for he was silent for a minute after he had moved the lamp.

Rosie looked him up and down. His presence didn't frighten her. No burglar would arrive on the job dressed in a dark suit and stylish wide-shouldered overcoat. Anyway, Luscombe didn't suffer from crime. No one had been burgled for years, certainly not in the winter when there were no tourists about and the locals were around to keep an eye on the place. A new bit of graffiti on the bus shelter was about all the crime that ever happened in this part of the world. And what self-respecting burglar would walk into a house via the front door and head for the only room with a light on in the entire house?

'I'm Hal Dickinson.' He nodded towards the bed, and Rosie had the full benefit of his wonderfully handsome profile, delicate yet unyieldingly firm. 'This is my father. I take it you must have come in from the village to give my sister a hand. She's been getting quite exhausted.'

'Yes, I come in four nights a week to give Mrs Sutherland some help,' Rosie murmured, rising stiffly to her feet.

'You're not a Macmillan?' Hal Dickinson's voice held an undertone of disbelief that Rosie should be helping anyone out. She smoothed her hair and looked up at him with flustered eyes, and despite his initial distaste at her, so bulky and silly, he noticed with a shock the gentle intelligence in her eyes, and the atmosphere of unhappiness that surrounded her.

'No, I'm not a Macmillan. I haven't had the specialised training. Though I wouldn't mind going in for it,' she added quickly, lest he should think her arrogant or unenthusiastic about caring for the terminally ill. Macmillan nurses were specially trained in all aspects of cancer care and provided by a cancer charity. They were marvellous—and very thin on the ground.

'I'm to take it that you have *some* form of specialised training, though?' Hal's eyebrow rose sceptically. She didn't look like any nurse *he'd* ever known.

'Oh yes, I'm an SRN. I've had years of experience at a big London hospital, Highstead, so I'm not a complete beginner.' She tried to laugh casually, but the sound came out hoarsely in the silent night and just made her feel even more stupid. 'Did you say that Mrs Sutherland is your sister?' Rosie added, desperate for something to say, something to distract him from his disbelieving study of her.

'My half-sister, by my father's first wife. My mother was his second wife—which goes to explain why Phyllis is so many years my senior.' He smiled knowingly at Rosie through the gloom. 'Does that answer all your questions, Nurse?'

'I didn't . . .' Rosie looked at her feet and noticed a ladder creeping up from the top of one foot of her tights. Sometimes she could feel good and look good; and sometimes, like today, nothing in the world went right and whatever she did was bound to make things worse.

'How's Father?' Hal drew close to the bed and Rosie could see how the angular bones of the old man were echoed in the sharp good looks of his son. Before she could launch into the 'he's as well as can be expected' routine, he interrupted her. 'And don't give me any soft soap. I'm a GP; I know what's happening and I know what all the jargon means.'

Underlying his harsh tone and the brisk, careless words, Rosie was aware of something deeper. He must be upset, she realised, watching him as he raised his father's limp hand and took the pulse before smoothing the white forehead. 'It's really just a matter of pain control now,' she said quietly, going to stand by his side and feeling the magnetic pull of his athletic body as she did so. 'As you know, there's nothing that can be done for him. He has morphia when he needs it—Dr Hills, the local GP, believes in total control, so your father isn't in any discomfort. I come most nights and the district nurse makes a call most days.'

Hal absorbed the information silently. Then suddenly he spoke in low, distant tones. 'He was always such an active man, always walking or riding, even when all this first started. I don't think he'd ever had a day in bed in his life before . . .' He sighed and picked up the old man's hand again.

Rosie restrained herself from reaching out and patting him on the shoulder. This man wasn't asking for sympathy and he wouldn't welcome it. There was something very tough in him, she knew instinctively. He seemed made of sprung steel. When he walked and moved it was with the force and grace of someone who knew exactly what he was doing and where he was going. His momentary sadness was quite understandable, particularly at this time of the morning and after a drive of God knew how many miles.

She stepped quietly back, leaving them together. When he turned round the dark eyes, seeming to glow in the pale expanse of his face, cast an amused look in her direction, as if her reticence and tact were funny to him. 'Perfect bedside manners, I see,' was all he said. Then he pointed to the vacuum jug on the tray, as if to change the subject. 'Is whatever's in there still hot?'

Rosie felt the slight go home, and even though she knew that he must be upset, she couldn't quite bring herself to forgive him. Men like Hal Dickinson, good-looking, vital, dynamic, liked to pretend that women like her didn't exist. In their idealised world there was room for only one kind of woman —a beautiful one, who shared their preoccupations. Rosie had been on holiday to the South of France a couple of years ago with nursing friends, but she'd hated it there, because everyone, even her nursing chums, had blossomed and become beautiful in that beautiful place. Everywhere they had gone, men and women of incredible affluence and good looks had surrounded them. Rosie, sunburned and plump in her boring cotton frocks, had never felt so self-conscious or ignored in her life. And here was another virtual stranger making her feel just as awful.

'It's coffee. I expect it's still hot,' she murmured with embarrassment. 'I'll have to go down to the kitchen and get you another cup. I wasn't told to expect visitors.'

'I don't want to inconvenience you,' he said with a touch of sarcasm. 'You're not suffering from anything contagious, are you?'

'No!' Rosie wasn't sure what he was implying, but she didn't like the way he settled himself in her chair and flicked the remains of her doughnut away with his finger.

'I'll use your cup then—if you don't mind? There's no need to go blundering down into the kitchen and waking everyone up, is there?'

Swallowing her feelings, which were beginning to be anything but pleasant, Rosie dutifully poured a cup of coffee and handed it to him, offering milk and sugar and seeing the glint in his eyes when he firmly and pointedly declined both. Oh well, of course he would. Wasn't he too perfect to be true? And wasn't he sitting there, the epitome of glowing good health, rejecting all temptations that mortals couldn't turn down? He had her at a huge disadvantage and he was doing nothing to alleviate her shyness and embarrassment. He couldn't be a very nice person to behave in such a manner. Doctors usually had a good word for nurses, but not Hal Dickinson. Maybe it was all part of his toughness.

Fondly, Rosie thought back to Sister Slater. She would have known what to say and do to bring this man down a peg. She'd send him packing with a stern warning that his presence was not welcome in the sick room and that he could take his cool-as-a-cucumber derision elsewhere. But Rosie knew that she could never do that. She stood uncomfortably by the table as he drank his coffee. One of his long, lean fingers flipped open the magazine at the page she had been reading.

For a moment he seemed to digest the contents in silence. Then, with unconcealed delight, he began to read aloud. 'Jade felt the pressure of Hakim's hands as he ran them over her shoulders, down the small of her back, up again, and began to undo the ties of her bikini. "Stop!" she tried to murmur, but her breath came out on a sigh as his hands, covered now in sun oil, reached around her . . . "I will not stop, my darling," Hakim breathed softly in her ear, "until you know what it is like to experience all my love . . ."'

Hal glanced up and saw Rosie scarlet with confusion. He had gone too far with his teasing, he knew. She wasn't the big, bouncing, buxom village girl he'd first thought her. There was something sensitive and touching about her, something that prevented him from laughing her off as he did so many silly girls. 'Good night, Nurse.' He rose abruptly to his feet, a grin on his face. 'Enjoy the rest of the story. I'm going to find a bed and have some *very* pleasant dreams.' Still laughing, he left her.

*   *   *

The problem with men like Hal Dickinson, Rosie mused, as she gave his father his early-morning wash, was that they were so confident and unshakeable that it would take an absolute superhuman to impress them. Someone ordinary, someone *very* ordinary like herself, was absolutely nothing to them. Not, she sniffed with mild defiance, that she wanted Hal Dickinson to take any notice of her. But if he was around and they were going to have to meet again at some point, she didn't want to be on the receiving end of his amused reproof. He looked at her as if he'd never seen anything like her before in his life; as if she was a lower form of life that intrigued him in a quaint sort of way, and it hurt.

Mr Dickinson gave a slight groan as she laid him gently back against the pillows. It seemed a pity, Rosie thought soft-heartedly, to move him about when he was so ill. She held his bony hand between her pink ones and stroked it caringly. 'It's all right, Mr Dickinson,' she whispered, unsure of whether he could hear her or not. Morphia dulled the senses and confused people, and it was very likely that he had no idea of what was going on—but there was no harm in a little tenderness. 'Your son's come to see you today,' she went on, pulling the sleeve of his pyjama jacket up to give him his morning injection of the pain-killing drug. 'That'll be nice for you, won't it?'

The first sounds of the day were beginning. Outside the cows were beginning to moo as they were herded in for first milking, and the occasional car could be heard in the direction of the village's main street. A bath was being run in the bathroom and Rosie could hear Mrs Sutherland's voice talking to someone. Maybe her brother's arrival was as much a surprise for her as it had been for Rosie.

Rosie placed the used syringe in its special marked bag, to be disposed of with care, and began to tidy the room, putting the cup and vacuum jug on the tray and packing away her magazines and book and the incriminating remains of the doughnut that Hal Dickinson had caught her eating red-handed. She blushed as she thought of how he must have found her, fast asleep and sprinkled with sugar, like some irresponsible student nurse, exhausted after a night out with a boy-friend. No wonder he had found her so funny! And then when he had woken her up by turning the lamp on, she must have sat there gawping blindly like some ruffled, plump owl . . . She watched her cheeks redden in the mirror above the fireplace and took in her wayward wavy brown hair that stood out untidily all round her face. *Just* like a ruffled owl, with that wide placid face and soft expression.

'Nurse Simpson, I do hope your unexpected visitor didn't give you too much of a shock last night. He said you obviously weren't expecting him—I can't think what he meant by that, as *I* wasn't expecting him either!' Mrs Sutherland, resplendent in her serviceable blue tartan dressing-gown and with two pin-curls held in position on her cheeks with hairclips, entered the room in her usual bustling manner.

'Oh, did he——'

'I was expecting him this morning, but he decided to miss the traffic and come down overnight. It's a long enough drive as it is, without anyone else on the roads,' Mrs Sutherland commented vaguely. Rosie nodded agreement, having not the faintest idea how far Hal had driven—and rather wishing that he hadn't bothered. 'How has Father been?' Mrs Sutherland asked.

'He's spent a very quiet night. I've taken care of everything, so when the district nurse comes she won't have to wash him,' Rosie replied, a little embarrassed by Phyllis Sutherland's close scrutiny. All she wanted now was a clean getaway from this house, a decent breakfast and then a few hours in bed. 'He's had his first injection and he took a little water about midnight.'

'You're very good with him.' Phyllis looked the girl up and down with an enquiring eye. She was so shy, rather gauche for her age, yet there was something kind about her. If she made an effort to watch her weight and acquired a little confidence she would be charming.

'Why don't you go home a little early,' she said kindly.

'Thanks, that would be lovely, if you're sure you can cope.' Rosie was supposed to stay until eight and it was now only just gone seven-thirty. But she'd done more than was strictly her duty—and she wanted to avoid Hal if she possibly could.

'Of course I can.' Mrs Sutherland ushered her out on to the landing. 'We'll see you at around ten this evening, shall we, as usual? Hal will be here, of course, but he won't bother you.' With a familiar wave, she disappeared back into her own room to dress.

She was both right and wrong, Rosie thought reflectively as she went downstairs into the kitchen and out into the back porch of the old house, where she left her bicycle each night. Hal Dickinson certainly wouldn't bother her; not for her own sake, anyway. He obviously hadn't much relished her company in the early hours of the morning and it was unlikely that he would seek her out tonight for another uncomfortable silence. But he *did* bother her in another way. He was a man—a good-looking man. He would be enough to bother any woman with red blood in her veins. And Rosie was, she knew of old, especially vulnerable to men like that.

She loaded her canvas bag with its magazines, her knitting and her book, into the wicker basket that rode on the front of the bicycle, and began to wheel it out of the porch. It felt peculiarly heavy and ungainly. She bent to look at the front tyre.

'Blast!' It was flat.

'You've got a puncture by the look of it.' Hal Dickinson, more spare and darkly saturine than ever in the cold light of morning, stood looking down on her with that half-exasperated expression he'd worn the night before. He was wearing faded denims and a chunky misty blue sweater which emphasised the strong column of his throat and the length of slimly athletic legs.

'Yes, I can see that.' Rosie gulped. The way he looked and bore himself told so much about him —a healthy life, an active outlook. And what did she, plump and frumpy in her flat shoes and tan tights and silly white overall, represent? A lazy, self-indulgent existence. Embarrassment shook her. 'I'll push it home,' she muttered, and went to wheel it out into the garden again. Anything, anything at all, to escape him and his naturally supercilious air.

'There's no need to push it all the way home,' he said immediately, and restrained the bike by grabbing the rear mudguard and pulling against her. 'I can mend a puncture for you.' For another woman he might have sounded more eager. Rosie, though, picked up the mild exasperation lurking in his tone.

'It's all right,' she protested, dragging at the front. 'I can get home, thank you.'

'You can start cooking some breakfast and *I'll* fix this.' The steely glint in his eye told her that his mind was made up. 'I'll have bacon and eggs. My brother-in-law won't be down for another twenty minutes or so and Phyllis has gone to sit with Father for half an hour—and I'm starving.'

So that was it, Rosie thought as, with a confused nod, she squeezed back past him into the kitchen. He was hungry enough to exchange a puncture repair for breakfast. A straight barter, a business transaction. No personal pleasure or feelings involved. She felt increasingly like some despised sort of servant, tolerated but not very much liked.

He left the back door which led on to the little porch open as he worked, peeling off the tyre with strong fingers. Rosie found her way around the kitchen without much trouble, and he seemed to anticipate her questions, so that she didn't find much to say to him.

A splashing in the sink beside her roused her from her thoughts. Hal filled the bowl with water and then submerged the inner tube. A solitary bubble rose and popped on the surface.

'There's the culprit,' he murmured, and ran his finger over the spot where the bubble had come from. 'It's a thorn. You must have run over some rose trimmings or something on your way here. And can I have my bacon grilled?'

'Yes, of course.' Rosie refrained from telling him that she was going to grill it anyway. He obviously assumed that she was going to fry it in plenty of dripping. 'I am aware of the current debate about saturated and unsaturated fats,' she was stung to reply.

'Really?' He said it vaguely, disbelievingly, as he turned away, drying off the tyre. Rosie couldn't help but watch his broad back and think how good-looking he was. She felt her heart give a bump and turned back to the stove, where the bacon had begun to spit. Memories of Giles Levete and the fool she had made of herself over him came trickling back. Mr Levete had been kind to her, taken her out for a drink—but not because he was interested in her. No, he'd wanted to find out a bit more about Sister Slater, that was all. And on the strength of one night out with him and a friendly kiss on the doorstep she had fancied herself in love with him, had planned all sorts of adventures and a future . . .

'Tell me, how did that story finish last night? I lay awake for hours wondering what happened.' Hal, in the porch, finished sticking the patch over the hole in the inner tube and began to lever the tyre back into position. His teasing tone was torture to Rosie, who prodded the bacon as it began to spit under the grill and tried to pretend that she hadn't heard him.

'I don't know. I didn't bother reading it,' she mumbled. 'I'm not very keen on things like that.'

'An old-fashioned girl, eh?' With a snap the tyre bounced back into its rim. Hal uncurled himself without effort, righted the bicycle and stood up languidly. 'Is my breakfast ready yet?' he enquired as he came to the sink to wash his hands.

'Just done.' Rosie turned the eggs and bacon on to the plate she'd heated and piled toast high around the edge. It looked unbearably appetising and her stomach began a low rumble.

'Are you due to come again tonight?'

'Yes. I'll be here around ten.' Rosie didn't dare ask if he would still be here. Half of her hoped that he would, but that she could see him without having the difficulty of talking to him. The other half wished him in another county by nightfall.

'There's really no need. I can sit up with Father —and from the state I found you in last night, I imagine you could do with a proper night's rest.' Hal reached nonchalantly for the towel and pretended that he hadn't seen the shiver of nerves and rejection that ran down Rosie's arm as she placed the plate upon the table.

'I'd better come, all the same. It's my job,' she managed, distracted by the sight of his lean tanned forearms and smarting from the rudeness of his words. What did he dislike so much in her? She didn't ask for glowing friendship from him, but his constant ridicule was unbearable.

'If you insist.' He went to sit down at the kitchen table, at the place that Rosie had carefully laid for him. 'Have a safe journey home.' Dismissed, Rosie went out to the back porch and began to wheel her bicycle away. Tears at his inexplicable behaviour stung her eyes. If she had been a pretty young girl he would have flirted and asked her to stay for breakfast. If she had been a married woman he would have been polite and friendly. But she was neither, and so he felt he was allowed to be as offhand as he liked.

Watching her walk past the kitchen window, one hand smoothing her hair in that almost constant gesture, Hal felt an instant of remorse. He'd been cold to her, and it wasn't her fault. It was just that he didn't want this shy, rather sad young woman to start getting friendly. He'd had enough of lonely young women attaching themselves to him emotionally. Claire was bad enough, without this new one. All the same, there was something in those luminous dark eyes she turned on him that made him instantly regret his sarcasm. Why did women have to look on him as the solution to their problems? And why was he stupid enough to respond to them?

He heard the squeak of the front gate as Rosie wrestled with it, trying to hold it open and get the bike through at the same time—no mean feat. Without thought, Hal threw down his knife and fork and ran to the front door. From there it was only a few yards to the front gate, and he held it wide while she, puzzled, steered the old red bicycle through. 'I'll have this,' he announced with false sharpness in his voice as he took the magazine out of the top of her bag. 'I simply have to know what Jade and Hakim got up to.' He gave her a last cynical smile, which curled her toes, and, shaking with self-consciousness, Rosie mounted the bicycle and pedalled heavily away.

Hal watched, genuinely amused by her grace on the old machine as she set off at steady pace. Then he looked at the lurid magazine in his hand and went straight round to the dustbin to throw it away. What on earth had made him do that? Now Nurse . . . He didn't even know her name! Nurse Large, he would call her. Well, now Nurse Large would think him a complete fool and go home to tell everyone in the village that he was a boor and an idiot. And with total justification, too, he thought gloomily as he walked back to his cold breakfast.

*   *   *

'Rosie! Rosie!' Mrs Simpson, a neat woman in a country tweed skirt and beige cardigan, shook her daughter's shoulder, which was sticking out from under the duvet. 'Rosie, wake up! There's an emergency.'

'What?' With memories of another wakening not so long ago, Rosie sat up. Her long brown hair, so annoyingly wavy and untidy when she was trying to keep it neat in a bun, fell around her ripe shoulders. 'Did I hear you say there's an emergency? What time is it?'

'It's only just gone eleven. Here, put something on and come down.' Mrs Simpson riffled helplessly through a pile of discarded clothes on a straight-backed chair. 'You must have something clean here.'

'What's happened?' Rosie slipped out of bed and went to the wardrobe where she found an old corduroy smock dress, one which hid all her faults.

'It's Justin Bates down at the village store. He was slicing some bacon for a customer and he's taken his thumb right off. The doctor's not at home and we can't take him into the General while he's still bleeding heavily. Hurry up! The poor lad's in trouble!'

Rosie trotted along to the bathroom and pulled on her undies and dress. She was far too old to be getting dressed in front of her mother, but Mrs Simpson, used to living without her daughter for so long, didn't seem to realise the fact. She tended to treat Rosie as if she was still just a schoolgirl, unmindful of the twelve years that had passed, the seven years in London, the long hours of training.

'I'm not really supposed to race to emergencies,' Rosie explained as they left the house, carrying the first-aid kit. 'If Justin Bates dies or loses his hand because of something I do, I'll be in terrible trouble.'

'You're a nurse, aren't you?' Mrs Simpson looked shocked. 'If you're a nurse, surely you have to go to the aid of anyone in distress?'

'Not if they really need the attention of a doctor. Simply because you're a nurse doesn't mean that you have the answer to everything, you know.' She didn't add that, as far as she was concerned, Justin Bates could suffer for a bit. Every time she went to the shop he started talking animatedly about diets and how terrible it must be to be fat to whoever would listen. He could only be about seventeen, Rosie reckoned, but he knew how to hurt people's feelings, and for some strange reason he'd taken against her from the first day she'd arrived in the village to stay with her parents. Maybe it was because during her time away she'd lost her local accent. Or because he resented the fact that she'd come from London and he'd never been there. Anyway, though Rosie didn't wish him any major ill, she didn't feel like racing to his aid.

'Here she is!' Mrs Simpson called proudly as they entered the shop. At the back of it, around the area where Justin carved ham and sliced bacon, a little crowd of people had gathered. They turned expectantly to Rosie, and she tried to hold her head high and exude confidence as she stepped forward.

Justin looked balefully up at her as she came to his side and took his hand, which was swathed in a teatowel. 'I've cut the end off the index finger,' he said manfully, 'and it's agony.'

'Poor lad,' sympathised one of the women, who

rather admired his adolescent brashness and took his cheek to be charm.

'Let's have a look. If anyone's squeamish, they'd better stand back. I don't want to have them fainting.' No one stood back. Curious, they all came forward, and recoiled again as Rosie lifted the makeshift bandage and the finger began to bleed again. 'Come and run it under the tap,' she instructed, and led the boy over to the sink where he washed his equipment. 'Don't touch anything, we don't want an infection. Just stand there with it under the tap for a minute. Was the teatowel clean?'

The shopkeeper assured her that it was. Justin stood sullenly at the sink, no longer the centre of attention now that Rosie had arrived. A closer inspection of Justin's finger revealed that far from slicing a chunk off himself, the lad had taken off only the very end of the finger. Rosie wrapped it in gauze while Justin held it high and assured the concerned ladies that although the pain was terrible, he'd be all right.

'I'm not going to give you anything for it, just in case they want to do something at the hospital,' Rosie told him as she finished. 'You'll have an anti-tetanus jab and they might give you some antibiotic, too, as you were working with meat. But if you can hold out without a pain-killer for a bit longer, it might help.'

Suddenly there was a commotion in the crowd and one or two people stood back to let a tall, dark-haired figure step forward. 'What on earth are you up to now?' Hal Dickinson asked incredulously, as he took in the sight of Rosie, hair still messed around her face and sleep still in her eyes, tending to Justin, who was sitting on the counter with his finger poking in the air. 'Is this where you usually hold surgery?' That same laughing glint was back and Rosie felt her self-confidence ebb away.

'Justin sliced off the end of his finger,' she said carefully. 'But it's all right, it's quite clean, and he can go off to Swanhill General now.'

'If it's clean, why bother sending him to hospital? Wait a second, I'll get my bag out of the car.' Hal left them for what seemed like seconds, then returned with his black leather bag. 'Here, let me have a look.' He elbowed Rosie aside and snipped off her carefully-applied bandage with sharp scissors.

'What do you think, Doc?' Justin asked cheekily. 'She seemed to know what she was doing, but you're the expert.'

'*Seemed!*' Rosie's indignation broke surface. 'I've dressed wounds you wouldn't be able to look at!'

'I'm sure you have,' Hal murmured, peering at the fingertip. 'And this is very clean and neat indeed. That's one thing about bacon slicers, they do a good job. No nasty tears.' He grinned up at Rosie, and for a moment they were both united in dislike of Justin. 'I'll give you a couple of jabs and a pain-killer, and then I suggest that you go home for the rest of the day and get over the incident. With any luck, young man, your finger will grow back again, nail and all, so you won't be any the worse for the accident. It's a good job that you didn't take any more off.'

'Grow back?' someone in the audience, who had watched Hal's performance admiringly, asked. 'You're having us on, aren't you, Doctor?'

Rosie was silent. She'd heard reports about how limbs and fingers could grow back as they had been, as long as they weren't badly damaged, but she'd never been absolutely sure whether it was totally true or not. She didn't want to show her ignorance in front of Hal, and she didn't want to be seen agreeing with him if it was only a fringe belief.

'No, I'm not. If we leave the finger unrestricted as soon as it's begun to heal, and if Justin takes care to keep it supple, it could very well grow back. He hasn't damaged any major nerves or muscles. You'd agree with the prognosis, wouldn't you, Nurse?' Hal's eyes were the darkest blue Rosie had ever seen, she thought as she faced him and he waited for her reply. Almost navy, they were so dark and mesmerising. 'Surely you've read the Galway report in last month's *Nursing Times*?' He looked more amused than ever at her discomfiture.

'No, I haven't,' she murmured lamely. 'But I must say that I've never seen any re-growth.'

'You disappoint me, Nurse. Now all these good people will think that I'm a quack.' Hal didn't seem too dismayed at the idea. He seemed, in fact, to find the gawping curiosity of what was by now almost half the village, amusing.

'I'm very sorry, Doctor.' From somewhere Rosie found the nerve to look him in the eye, and her voice was filled with the cool amusement that he seemed to find in her. Instantly she noticed surprise, then a shutter of distance close over his face.

'I'll take Justin somewhere a little more private for his jabs,' he said clearly, to the onlookers. 'And I think you can safely go back to your bed, can't you, Nurse?'

'I'll leave everything in your hands.' Rosie

snapped the lid of her meagre first-aid box and walked defiantly out of the shop. If he wanted to humiliate her on her own patch, he could. He had the upper hand in everything he did. Not only was he a doctor and she a nurse, but he had the natural authority and appearance that people took notice of. If they needed someone for an emergency, most of them, she knew, would be happy with her. But given the choice of who to side with, who wouldn't prefer the charismatic Dr Dickinson? Which made it all the more unfair, she thought bitterly as she climbed into bed and tried to fall back to sleep, that he should abuse his authority when she was around.

CHAPTER TWO

IT was a beautifully crisp March day, the sun brilliant over the daffodils that had forced their way up around the roots of the old trees that were clustered around the church. For a few minutes, as she walked up the path and surveyed the glorious scene, sunlight glowing on the mellow stone and the grass fresh and growing again, Rosie felt her heart lift—and then she remembered why she was here today and, worse, what it might mean to her.

In the church porch, Mr and Mrs Sutherland were waiting to enter, surrounded by relatives and village folk who had come to pay their last respects at the memorial service. Rosie hung back for a second, not because of them but because she could see a tall, dark-suited figure in front of them. And though it might not be Hal Dickinson, she didn't want to risk it. He had been less than kind to her before. What would he say now that his father had died, albeit quite expectedly?

Mr Dickinson's death had meant more than the end of her job, even though it had been upsetting. After all, she had nursed him for nearly nine weeks, and she felt in her own way that she had become close to him. But it wasn't just that. She'd felt sadness many times before when a patient had died, despite all her care. Somehow his death had marked the end of one short phase of her life and the beginning of another. She couldn't explain it. It was as if, in some way, she had needed an extended

break from her life at Highstead; a time to think
and decide for the future. And although as far as
she was aware she hadn't come to any major de-
cisions, she felt sure that the time had come to leave
home again and look for something elsewhere. But
what? That was the problem, she thought gloomily
as she entered the church and found a pew near the
back.

Rosie was still deep in thought when someone jogged her elbow. 'Nurse Simpson. Nurse
Simpson. Dreaming again?' Hal Dickinson's navy
eyes fell on her startled face as she looked up. 'My
sister has asked if you would come to the front of
the church. She doesn't want you sitting at the back
here, on your own.' He held out his arm with
studied courtesy, and although she had never
leaned on a man's arm before in her life, Rosie
instinctively threaded her own through. Hal lead
her down the aisle towards the front pews where
the family were sitting.

'I'm sorry about your father,' Rosie faltered, for
it had just occurred to her that if they swapped
arms, they would be proceeding down the aisle like
a bride and groom on their way to the altar. The
thought drove everything else out of her head. All
she was aware of was the firmness of his shoulder
against her and the way they had automatically
fallen into step. She could feel the warmth of his
body through the charcoal grey suit he wore and
feel the slight brushing of his thigh against hers. She
swallowed but found that her throat was dry.

'It's not such a terrible shock,' Hal replied, looking down at her. 'And your help has made the
whole thing so much easier for the family. We're all
very grateful, you know. Phyllis has been telling me

about how you stayed with her all last week, just keeping an eye on Dad.'

'I wouldn't have been happy, going off and leaving him.' Her words came out so cracked that for a moment Hal thought that she was overcome with grief and was going to cry.

'Why don't you sit here?' He led her to the far end of the front pew and placed her beside a middle-aged woman in a fancy hat that drifted with dyed ostrich feathers. In the slight draught from the stained-glass window the feathers bobbed and wafted like tufts of grass in a high wind. Phyllis Sutherland leant across this woman and said warmly,

'We couldn't have you sitting at the back there, out of things. Not after all you've done. I hope Hal has been nice to you. Apparently he was less than a perfect gentleman last time you met. You really shouldn't have cooked him breakfast.'

So that was why he'd been so pleasant, so quick with his praise, Rosie thought rebelliously. He was just obeying orders, obviously. She felt her cheeks colour with confusion. What had he thought of her, taking his arm so readily? She pulled away quickly and sat down—only to find that his arm, seemingly attached to hers, pulled heavily.

'I'm hooked!' He suppressed a laugh—they were, after all, in church.

'Oh dear, it's . . .' Rosie fiddled with the safety-chain of her watch-strap, which had somehow got itself hooked around the button on the cuff of his jacket. Her hands brushed his as they both tried to twist out of the knot, and she felt again that sensation, not unlike a static shock but completely pleasurable, suffuse her. The organ music, which had until now been meandering dolefully up and down the scales in the background as the organist waited for the congregation to arrive, suddenly burgeoned into life. Rosie had a sudden moment of panic that the vicar would appear and start the service as she and Hal Dickinson tugged away.

The same thing had occurred to him, for he instructed in an irritated voice, 'You'd better move along, Aunt Beatrice. I'll have to sit by Nurse Simpson for the service.'

The lady in the hat obligingly moved up a few inches, and Hal squeezed in beside Rosie. 'If you'd just hold still for a moment,' Rosie pleaded, trying to pry the button away from the wool fabric of the suit, 'I can pull it off.'

'Don't you dare!' The words were whispered through gritted teeth. 'Just sit still and wait until the service is over.'

And so they sat there while the service began. When the hymns were announced, Hal held the hymn-book and Rosie held her arm in the air, at the side of his. When the time came to kneel they completed the manoeuvre only with difficulty, and not before her hand had grazed his thigh so firmly that she began to wish a thunderbolt would strike them both for being so disrespectful. Could anything more embarrassing ever have happened to anyone? She couldn't look him in the face, fearful of what fury she might see there. Yet when, on struggling to their feet again, she caught his eye she found it full of wry amusement.

'I'm so sorry,' she breathed. 'This is terrible.'

'I think my father would have enjoyed it, all the same,' he whispered, and the smile he gave her was full of encouragement.

Somehow they succeeded in getting through the service without dropping anything or making too much fuss. Rosie was consumed with guilt that it wasn't Mr Dickinson Senior she was thinking about. No, it was his son who occupied her thoughts as they sat together, so inextricably linked. No matter how hard she tried to make herself concentrate on the vicar's words, or the short memorials of his friends and business colleagues, Rosie couldn't drive the dominating awareness of Hal Dickinson from her mind. He, for his part, and rightly, seemed to have forgotten her presence, and their predicament. As the service came to a close and the sonorous tones of the organ filled the air again, she breathed a sigh of relief.

Hal bent over and tried again to untangle his sleeve from Rosie's wrist, and within seconds the knot slipped loose and they could once again put a reasonable distance between themselves. Rosie wasn't slow to take note of the way that he immediately got to his feet, as if not to spend a moment longer in her presence. Well, she couldn't blame him. He'd made as light as he could of an upsetting incident. She should just be thankful for that.

'You'll come back to the house and have a cup of tea, won't you?' Mrs Sutherland asked.

'Oh, I wouldn't like to intrude.' The last thing Rosie wanted was to have to go back to the house and sit under Hal's scrutiny again, but Mrs Sutherland wouldn't take no for an answer.

'It's not as if it's the funeral itself,' she said staunchly. 'That was all over on Wednesday. Please come. You've become like one of the family over the past few weeks.'

'Well, if you insist, maybe I'll come along and have a cup of tea,' Rosie agreed.

'Good. Hal will give you a lift.'

They sat together in his sporty Golf outside the church, Rosie crammed in the back seat, while Aunt Beatrice said lengthy farewells to old acquaintances in the church porch. Mrs Sutherland and her husband and two other relatives had already gone ahead to the house. Rosie cleared her throat noisily and watched Hal's eyes swivel towards her in the driving mirror.

'I hope I'm not causing you any inconvenience.'

'None at all. It's Aunt Beatrice I'm waiting for. I'm only sorry to keep you waiting,' he replied courteously.

'Oh, I don't mind. I didn't even expect to be invited back to the house.' Everything she said seemed so feeble, Rosie thought dejectedly, trying to make a little more room for her knees and failing. The back of Hal's head was very attractive, with short dark curls springing over his collar. His jawline, she could just see the left side, was very strong, but then, she didn't need telling about his strong personality. She'd already been on the receiving end of it.

'Have you got another job lined up?' he asked suddenly, and she found his eyes on her again. She met his gaze and felt a flicker of heat rising inside her.

'No, I don't know what I'll be doing next. I've been lucky over the last couple of months with all the private work I've been able to pick up, but it's all dropped off recently.' Well, it hadn't dropped off, exactly; all her patients had died—but that didn't sound too good.

'How about the General? Do you want to go back into a hospital?' He voiced the question that Rosie had been asking of herself for the last few days, with no satisfactory answer. She had to do something, she knew. She couldn't stay at home for the rest of her life, picking up a little private work here and there. And her mother and she just didn't get on well enough these days for her prolonged visit home to go on for much longer. But what should she do? It wasn't even just a matter of making up her mind, for unemployment problems made finding *any* job difficult these days . . .

'I really don't know,' she said honestly, and followed it up inadvertently with a big sigh. 'I don't want to stay here really, so going to the General isn't a good idea—even if they've got a suitable job going.' Hal seemed to be looking at her with a thoughtful expression on his face, but he didn't say anything. 'And I don't really want to go back to London right now. It's so big, and sometimes I used to feel so lost there.' There was a pause.

'Surely, though, a job in some country hospital would be boring after your years at Highstead? You've become used to dealing with a lot of specialised cases and big wards. You'd be like a big fish in a little . . .' He seemed to realise how hurtfully his words might be interpreted and finished the phrase with a discreet cough. 'What I mean is, from what I've seen of you, you seem to enjoy a challenge, using your own initiative. And you wouldn't get much chance for that in some cottage hospital.'

'I hadn't really thought of myself as a big fish, but I don't suppose I'd enjoy life on a small ward in a small place,' Rosie agreed, wondering what he was getting at. Did he really think that she was the sort to want a challenge? It was the last picture in which she could see herself, but maybe to an outsider it did look that way. After all, she'd quite happily come down here, walked into strangers' houses and taken over the care of seriously ill people. She cast her mind back over her years on Sister Slater's ward at Highstead. Come to think of it, she'd carried an awful lot of responsibility on her shoulders. Naturally, when Sister was there she had given the orders. But there were plenty of times when she had been off the ward and Rosie herself had taken charge of serious post-operative cases. And Sister had trusted her and let her get on with her own work without many questions or much supervision . . .

A small glow of achievement began to suffuse her. She'd never really thought of herself as much of a success at anything in the past; she'd never had an exciting life, and she was always one to underestimate her own capabilities. Hadn't Sister Slater told her that herself, when she'd urged her to apply for a Sister's post or get more experience elsewhere? Yet things had been pleasant with Sister – pleasant, that was, until Mr Levete had come upon the scene—and she hadn't wanted to leave her cosy corner. Most nurses had found Sister bossy and too much of a perfectionist; Rosie suddenly began to see that the reason they had got on so well together for so long was that, in some almost indefinable way, they shared a skill and a dedication, even if their personalities had been different. For the very first time, sitting in the back of Hal Dickinson's car, she began to realise that Sister had valued and trusted her because she *was* a good nurse; the sort who liked a challenge and used her initiative.

'So you really don't know what you're doing?'
Hal asked reflectively, but his mind too seemed to
be far away, and his question wasn't the sort that
required a response. Aunt Beatrice's arrival
surprised them both, and after they had helped
her into the car, and found a place for her large
handbag and her umbrella, they set off for the
Sutherlands' house, Hal driving smoothly but with
surprising speed. Rosie sat in the back thinking for
the five-minute duration of the journey. She might
not have found an answer to all the questions she
had been asking herself, but it felt as if a light bulb
had been switched on in her life. Hal Dickinson
thought she was resourceful and needed a challenge, and that counted for a lot.

Such thoughts were still buzzing in her brain as
she excused herself from the gathering in the
Sutherlands' sitting-room and went out to the
kitchen to see to the washing-up. Aunt Beatrice
and a couple of the other elderly visitors had begun
to be a little tearful after the photo albums were
brought out, and Rosie herself felt rather upset by
pictures of Mr Dickinson in his heyday. The fact
that she didn't know him well had allowed her to
weather his death without upset, yet now she felt
that she was beginning to get involved with the
family. Hal had sat quietly on the other side of the
room, drinking tea and talking to his brother-in-law
but seeming distant in some way, as if he were
thinking deeply about something.

She dried the teacups and set them out in a
gleaming row on the kitchen table. Maybe this was
the last time she would come to this house. Maybe
this was the last time she would see Hal Dickinson.
After all, they'd both been connected with the

village for years and they'd never had anything to do with each other before now . . .

The door behind her opened and he entered the kitchen. She didn't see him for a moment, intent on her work, and he took in her calm manner and the aura of shyness that seemed to surround her. He feared that he was making a grave mistake, and yet there was something in her that he knew was just right for his purposes. And despite her apparent softness and lack of confidence, he felt that at heart she was tougher and more capable than she appeared. If he should have made the wrong decision, he knew it might be a total disaster.

'Nurse Simpson, how would you like to come and have a stroll round the garden with me?' he asked casually.

Her look, startled and suspicious, made him add an explanation. 'There's something I want to talk to you about. I have a proposition to make—about work.'

Dumbly Rosie nodded and followed him out through the back porch into the large, rambling garden that Mrs Sutherland never quite succeeded in taming. They strolled along the path in single file, the grass still being very damp, and Rosie felt pleased that her only black shoes, which she'd had to wear today, had low heels that didn't catch between the bricks.

What could he possibly want to talk about? Maybe he had a contact with someone at the local hospital. Maybe he had a suggestion to make about further training. They reached the vegetable garden, well away from the house, where the path broadened and they were able to stand side by side. She could sense his unease. Whatever he was going to say, it wasn't something he felt sure about—she could see that by the troubled look in those navy eyes and the flicker of a frown on his broad forehead. His face, so handsome and intelligent, thrilled her. It wasn't often she had the pleasure of the company of such a good-looking man, even if he was only going to discuss business with her.

'Have you ever thought about general practice?' His question caught her out; did he think she ought to be a doctor? 'I mean, have you ever thought of becoming a nurse in a general practice?'

'No, not really,' she admitted honestly. 'I did once think of doing my Community, but I wasn't sure I'd like all the travelling and the constant problems. Sorry,' she added apologetically.

'I'd better explain my reasons for asking,' Hal said carefully, reaching out and pinching an early bud from one of the overhanging branches. 'As you may or may not know, I'm in general practice. In the past year I've moved into a small local health centre with another GP. It's quite a rural area, but we're well-used, and we've decided to look for a nurse to help with the work.'

'Oh.' Rosie's voice gave away her disappointment. She didn't want to be a GP's nurse-cum-receptionist at some out-of-the-way health centre, supervising examinations and setting out patients' notes. If he thought she was looking for a challenge in that direction, he'd got it wrong.

'Not an ordinary surgery nurse, but a nurse who'd run her own side of the centre,' Hal hastened to correct her. 'We need someone to deal with all the minor and practical things that come in, of course—cuts and burns and blisters—but also someone to run the ante-natal clinics and work in tandem with our health visitor and community nurse. It would be quite a responsible position, and if you wanted to go on from there to doing something bigger . . .'

'Like what?' Rosie's curiosity had been captured now. He made the place sound more interesting than the average GP practice.

'Well, there's a new scheme for nurses to take on some of the doctors' responsibilities—the Nurse Practitioner training. And we're all very forward-looking in the practice, you won't find anyone difficult to work with. We'd hope that after a while with us you had the confidence and the expertise to start up your own schemes for the centre.'

'Have my own practice, that kind of thing?' It did sound fascinating, Rosie had to admit. And it would certainly solve some of her present problems. But could she bear to work with Hal Dickinson for long? She looked at him again, and he seemed less fierce and sardonic than he had before. Maybe that night he'd woken her up he'd been tired after his journey. And, naturally, he'd been very worried and upset about his father. Perhaps she ought not to blame him for his bad temper and sharpness with her. After all, she'd done nothing to inspire his confidence.

'You would have your own surgery, with all facilities. And we have two assistants, one of them a half-trained nurse who does all the basic super-visionary work around the centre, so you wouldn't be lumbered with all the administration.' Hal smiled as he watched the idea growing on her. The fact that she hadn't immediately jumped at the idea was reassuring in some way. It showed him that she wasn't desperate to take anything that would get her away from here and the dead-end that she seemed to have landed herself in. Claire had jumped at the idea when he'd suggested that she might like to work at the centre, and look what had happened then. His spirits rose a fraction. He *did* hope Rosie would take the job. She might be funny and look less than enticing, but there was something reassuring and uncomplicated about her.

'What sort of hours would it be? And what sort of salary? And just where is it?' Rosie wasn't going to be pressured into anything by a pair of melting navy eyes and the slightest hint of a smile.

Hal named a figure that was a little more than she had been earning in London as a senior staff nurse, and hours which would have made her old job look a doddle. 'It's in Suffolk,' he added. 'Do you know it at all?'

'No.' Rosie shook her head. 'Is it nice?'

Hal laughed long and hard. 'Yes, it's very nice indeed. Not too far from the coast, and with lots of trees and fields, so you as a country girl won't feel too hemmed in. But we've a couple of good-size towns not far away, and you can get to London easily enough, if you want to see your old friends. What do you say?'

'I'll need to think about it,' Rosie replied steadily, though in truth her mind was made up, and as much by his interest in her and that smile as by the promises of the job itself. 'If I were to say yes, wouldn't your partner need to have a look at me before I joined?'

Her face clouded a little, for she knew how unprepossessing she was to look at. It had been the bane of her life at Highstead. No new doctor ever took much notice of her, not for months, assuming that she was slow and a bit stupid too. Nor could she pretend to enhance the surroundings of his clinic. It was all very well to say that, yes, she would take the job, but what if the other members of the clinic didn't like the look of her?

'If I say that you're right for the job, they'll accept my decision,' Hal said firmly, sensing that something had worried her. A pretty nurse or receptionist, he knew, might draw unwanted attention. Pretty young girls had boy-friends—and boy-friend trouble. They stayed out late at night and took the next day off work. But Rosie . . . Well, Rosie was the reliable kind; he knew that much from his dealings with her here and his sister's reports. It was unlikely that Rosie would get into trouble. She was one of those plain, simple but efficient career nurses. One of those who, if given too much rope, turned into crusty old battle-axes, the backbone of the hospital and curse of her staff. A twinge of guilt hit him for writing her off so easily, but surely no man could ever take Rosie Simpson seriously in a romantic way? Well, *he* didn't.

'If I was to accept your offer, when would you want me to start?' Rosie's brown eyes were upon him. She must, she knew, steel herself against him. If she once began to feel about him the way she'd felt about Giles Levete, there would be terrible trouble.

'Today is Friday. I'll give you the weekend to think it over. Call me at this number on Monday and let me know what you think.' He handed her a card with an impressive-sounding address and telephone number on it. 'Obviously it depends on how long you'll need to get things set up, but maybe you could start the Monday after that.' He turned on his heel and began to walk away up the garden path. 'I'll let you have a think about it out here.'

With the card in her hand, Rosie nodded silently and watched him go. What on earth was she going to do?

CHAPTER THREE

THE train drew slowly into Woodbridge station. The light was failing and Rosie couldn't make out many details of the countryside they passed, except that it seemed watery and different to her recent Devon surroundings. She began to wonder, as she gathered her heavy suitcases, whether this job was really a good idea. She had no idea about what she was coming to, other than a few vague promises from Hal Dickinson. In Devon, though, anything would have sounded attractive. What would it actually be like to live here?

'You'll be met at the station,' he'd said on the telephone. 'We'll fix some accommodation up for you. We'll expect you Sunday evening.'

It had been as simple as that. Perhaps too simple, Rosie thought ruefully as she threw her cases from the train and clambered down, breathless, after them. The place seemed practically deserted. There didn't seem to be anyone here to meet the train. Maybe it was all so simple that they'd forgotten her.

About a dozen people alighted with her, but none of them offered to carry her cases and, being local, they all rapidly dispersed in their own directions. Rosie felt her heart sink as she handed in her ticket to the collector on the gate and slowly, arms and hands protesting at the strain of her cases, made her way out to the car-park. At the far end of it was parked a car that looked, from this distance, remarkably like Hal's. Cursing under her breath, and wondering why he hadn't been decent enough to come to her aid, she made her way to it.

Just as she reached it, the driver's door opened and a blonde woman, dressed casually but very fetchingly in faded denims and a light sheepskin jacket, got out. 'You're not Nurse Simpson for the clinic in Clayburgh, are you?' she asked, and there was something almost disbelieving in her voice that set Rosie's teeth on edge.

'As a matter of fact, I am,' she admitted grimly, wondering at the same time whether it was too late to deny it all and head back to London.

'I'm sorry for not coming into the station to meet you.' The girl's face lit up with a charming smile, and Rosie felt herself smiling back, despite her less than warm feelings. 'I got here much too early, so I've been sitting listening to the radio in the car. I quite forgot the time. Here, let me help you with those.'

With a speed and strength that was belied by her rather pale pink-and-blonde looks, she took one of the suitcases and almost threw it into the hatchback of the vehicle. Rosie, labouring under the strain of the other, hoisted it in.

'I'm glad to see that you've come to stay,' the girl laughed. 'By the way, I'm Claire Kemp, an old friend of Hal's. He told me that he'd met you while you were nursing his father. I do hope you'll be very happy here with us.' She had a most disconcerting way, Rosie thought, of changing the tables on you—talking of one thing, then passing on to something else almost immediately.

'Yes, I met him down in Devon. And I'm pleased to meet you,' she replied, shaking hands and then moving round to the other side of the car to get in. Claire seemed to move very quickly, as well as talk and change the subject with speed. In fact, Rosie decided as the car moved swiftly away before she'd even had a chance to put her seatbelt on, we're like chalk and cheese—totally different, not a thing in common. It didn't seem a very good omen. If Claire was the sort of woman whom Hal made his old friend, what chance would she . . .

Stop it, she reminded herself sharply. There was no way a man like him could feel any interest in a woman like her, and it was foolish to even think of it. Comparisons were always odious, anyway. Certainly comparison to Claire Kemp, with her quick, alert manner and charming confidence was odious.

'Now,' Claire announced, swinging the car round a tight country corner and coming again to a stretch of road that ran along the bank of one of the creeks or rivers so numerous in this area, 'I'm going to take you to one of the local pubs. It's very comfortable—or so I've heard people say. You can stay there for a couple of days while you get your bearings and then you can move into the flat at the clinic—if you want to, of course.'

'That sounds fine,' Rosie responded. 'I didn't know there was a flat.'

'I don't think Hal wanted to mention it unless it was ready for you to move into—and it's not. Not yet, anyway,' Claire added quickly. 'We're getting the electricity and everything laid on next week, though, and as soon as that's done, you can move in.'

'Gosh!' Rosie's scepticism vanished as she saw behind her all the years in grotty digs with difficult landladies, or shared houses and flats with everyone running for the bathroom at the same moment. This job really did seem to have everything going for it, despite the possible drawback of Claire Kemp.

'We're coming into Clayburgh now. It's quite a large village and there are a surprising number of people around. But with the bus service practically gone and quite a few people without cars, they find it difficult to get into Woodbridge. So we're pretty busy. The clinic's off the High Street just up there.' Claire pointed up a side street, but it was too dark for Rosie to see anything.

'Are you involved with the clinic too?' she asked, wondering why her heart sank so firmly when Claire replied.

'Oh yes! I'm one of the receptionists. Didn't Hal tell you?'

Rosie shook her head as they parked the car outside a rather ordinary-looking pub and climbed out. It didn't seem to be the kind of place that anyone would recommend very highly. Just up the road there was a much nicer one, with bulbs in window boxes under its old mullioned windows and a cheerful glow coming from within. Rosie hoped for a few forlorn seconds that they would cross the road with her luggage and enter the welcoming one. But Claire was already humping one of her suitcases onto the doorstep of the other.

'I won't come in with you,' she said cheerfully, 'but Mr Hope is expecting you—I rang him this morning. He seemed a bit surprised, but then I don't suppose he gets a lot of guests at this time of year. You should be able to get a hot meal here, and we'll see you at the clinic tomorrow. Everyone around here knows the way.' And with a wave she was gone, back into the car and away.

Maybe, thought Rosie, staring at the peeling floral wallpaper of her tiny bedroom, Claire Kemp was staging a vendetta against her. If she *was* she was certainly going the right way about it. Mr Hope had clearly been a bit bemused at her arrival. He'd commented aloud that he hadn't had paying guests for ages, and he'd apologised for the state of her room. And when Rosie had asked whether she could get an evening meal in the bar, he'd looked most confused.

'We don't do what you'd call *proper* food here, miss,' he'd said roundly, scratching his head. 'I mean, we got crisps and pork pies, that kind of thing . . .'

After a whole day of British Rail pork pies and crisps, even Rosie could feel no enthusiasm for such fare. 'And could you show me the bathroom, please,' she'd remembered, just as he was about to leave.

'That's down the end of the landing.' He pointed down the long, cold corridor with its holey carpet and flaking walls. 'You'll be sharing it with me and the wife, mind. We're not fancy here.'

The bed was lumpy and so cold that it felt damp. Maybe it *was* damp, Rosie thought despairingly. What on earth was Claire Kemp up to, billeting her somewhere like this? Surely this couldn't have been her idea of a comfortable lodging? She opened one of her suitcases and took out her old blue uniform dress and a white apron that she had purposely packed on top. Of course, she didn't know for certain whether Hal Dickinson and his colleagues would want her in uniform, but it would be as well to turn up looking smart and official tomorrow. There was single rusty wire coat hanger in the utility-style wardrobe whose hinges creaked as if they'd last played in some Dracula film. And when she slid the dress onto the hanger and went to place it on the rail, there was a resounding crash as the hanging rail fell.

In the silence that followed the crash Rosie caught the scrabbling of clawed feet behind the skirting board and heard alarmed mice vanishing into the roof space or wherever they had come from. Mice! The very last thing she needed was an infested room . . . Tired, hungry, and beginning to suspect that this was the worst decision she had ever taken in her life, Rosie sank to her knees on the worn carpet and began to weep silent tears. It was too much. She had staked so much on this job, on a new start. And now . . .

Feet approaching along the dim corridor roused her. Whoever it was, they weren't a member of the Hope household, for they were stumbling in the holes in the carpet and giving out muted curses. Suddenly there was a loud knock on her door. 'Nurse Simpson? Rosie? Are you in there?' There was only one person with that voice. Hal Dickinson was here.

In a split second Rosie wiped her face as best she could and, uttering a muffled, 'Yes, I am. Come in,' opened the door to him.

'I'm afraid it's a bit scruffy and I haven't been able to unpack yet,' she apologised, for the room was in a state, with her baggage cluttering every spare inch that was not already crammed with nasty Formica-topped tables covered in cigarette burns, and wobbling chests of drawers.

'A good job too! What on earth are you doing here?' Hal was casually dressed in grey cord
trousers and a heavy Aran sweater, with a tweedy
jacket over the top. His voice and manner were,
however, anything but casual. 'You're supposed to
be staying at the Horse and Cart, not here, for
goodness' sake. How did you get into this hell-
hole?' He surveyed the room with obvious distaste
and plainly did not intend to enter it.

'Claire—Miss Kemp—brought me here. She'd
booked me a room. I was expected, though Mr
Hope did seem surprised,' Rosie admitted.

'She needs her brains testing, that girl. Honestly,
I told her that the Horse and Cart was the best pub
to put you up in—and she goes and gets you a room
here. No wonder the landlord was surprised, I
don't suppose he has anyone except the odd com-
mercial traveller who's willing to put up with this.
Come on we'll get you out of here and over the
road.' Rosie wasn't so slow that she had missed the
slight smile in his eye as he talked of Claire. And
despite the girl's blunder, he obviously wasn't too
angry with her. And Claire drove his car, too.
Maybe they lived together . . .

She rescued her dress from the bottom of the
wardrobe and folded it neatly into its case. There
was very little to pack up; she hadn't had the heart,
in her half-hour here, to do anything except worry
about how she was going to survive. Hal risked
entering the room to pick up the cases. Despite his
slimness, he seemed to have no trouble with them
both, and he clunked down the corridor, knocking
more paint from the peeling walls as he went. Rosie
followed behind, feeling foolish and slightly resent-

ful that he hadn't even bothered to apologise on Claire's behalf for the mistake. Surely it wasn't too much to ask that he try to say sorry?

Leaving her for a moment in the saloon bar, which was unoccupied, Hal went round to the other side of the partition, from which there came much raucous laughter and shouting. Rosie shivered. If she hadn't had the foresight to ask about food, she might have come tearing down here expecting a hot dinner—and from the sound of it, the locals would have been much amused by that!

'Right, I've squared it with Mr Hope. He wasn't very happy with the idea of having a "young lady" on the premises anyway, so he's not going to worry. We'll go over to the Horse and Cart. I expect they'll have a spare room for you.' And with that, Hal picked up her suitcases again and loped to the door. For her he'd had barely a word. Not so much as a 'How are you?' or a 'Hope you had a good journey.' The disappointment, quelled a little by his arrival, began to well again in Rosie's bosom.

But the Horse and Cart dispelled some of it. 'You've come off rather well from the mistake,' Hal laughed as he pushed open the door of her room. 'They've let all the singles, so you'll just have to make do with a double—and your own bathroom.'

'It must be ever so expensive . . .' Rosie bit her lip as she walked in behind him, for she hadn't bargained on such luxury living. The four-poster was hung with pretty drapes and the whole room was bright and fresh, with lots of pink and pale green wallpaper and mellow old pine furniture. And the bathroom, she noted as she peeped through the door behind Hal, was equipped with a shower *and* a bath in ivory-coloured porcelain.

'I must admit that we hadn't planned to put you up in the honeymoon suite,' Hal agreed, and there was laughter dancing in his eyes at her blushes. 'But as it was Claire's fault, I think she ought to make it right. Mr Hope was going to charge you five pounds a night for that nasty little room over at the Cock, so if you'd care to contribute that, we'll pick up the rest of the bill.'

'Well—that's very nice of you, if you don't mind. Maybe I . . .'

But Hal wasn't listening. He glanced at his watch. 'If you don't go down now you won't be in time for dinner. They close the food bar at eight out of season. And I expect you're starving after your journey.'

'I wouldn't mind something,' Rosie admitted gingerly. She remembered his attitude to food —particularly to her food—from their past encounters. She didn't want him to think that she was starving, though in truth she did feel very peckish.

'I'll come down with you and have a drink while you order your meal—a sort of welcome-to-Clayburgh drink.' He laughed dryly. 'I'm sorry about Claire. She really doesn't think at times. I don't suppose that she's been in either pub since she arrived here, but she should have known simply from the look of the place that the Cock wasn't one I would recommend.'

'I think she made the booking by phone. She couldn't have known how grotty it was,' Rosie heard herself saying pleasantly, all thoughts of a vendetta firmly in the past.

'She had only to look at the place when she dropped you off. And it wasn't even very polite of her to just drop you off in the street like that. Sometimes I wonder . . .' Whatever he had been about to wonder, he stopped himself and went to the door. 'Why don't you spend a few minutes tidying yourself? I'll be down in the bar when you're ready. Don't be too long, though.' With a friendly smile, he made his way down the stairs.

In the splendour of the bathroom, Rosie washed her hands and face, brushed her hair out and applied some pink lipstick. Nothing she could do would make the full moon of her face look sophisticated, but at least she could look tidy, she thought. She pulled one of her flowing smock dresses, a floral one, from her bag and, ignoring the creases, put it on. It was odd, she reflected as she made her way downstairs, how one's emotions could rise and fall so rapidly in the space of an hour or so. At one point she had found herself wondering whether she could go on with this job – and now she skipped down the stairs, surprisingly happy at the thought of sharing a drink with the elegant Dr Dickinson.

'I've had to order for you,' he greeted her across the bar. 'They were in rather a hurry to finish tonight. I'm sorry, they've got some sort of function in one of the other rooms and they're very rushed. I hope you can eat roast beef?'

'That would be lovely.' Rosie's stomach gave a tell-tale rumble.

'And just think, you would have had to go to bed hungry if I hadn't come along to find you,' he laughed. 'What will you drink?'

Rosie ordered a glass of white wine, and it was soon brought by the barman. He indicated a table laid with a snowy cloth and gleaming silver cutlery and they both seated themselves at it.

'Claire told me that she's a receptionist at the clinic,' Rosie faltered, uncomfortable at having to make conversation with Hal's eyes on her. She'd forgotten their power and just how dark they were in the week since she had last seen him. Now, with as much force as ever, she realised what an exceptionally attractive man he was.

'That's right.' Hal ran his finger round the rim of his glass, seeming to ponder something very deeply for a moment. 'Look, I might as well warn you about Claire, seeing as you have already been on the receiving end of her scatterbrained ways.' He paused, as if he found it difficult to find the words. 'She hasn't been at the clinic for very long. In fact she's working there because she's an old friend of mine and in need of a job. She did a year of nursing training, so she can be quite useful to have around the place, in fact. But she's sometimes absolutely brainless!' He looked up and grinned. 'She'd never do anything to harm so much as a fly, but as you've already found out to your cost, sometimes she's quite thoughtless. And that's something to bear in mind when you're at the surgery. The rest of us have had a while to become accustomed to her whys and wherefores, but you should be warned.'

'You make her sound a positive danger,' Rosie smiled, 'and she's not that, I'm sure.'

'I wouldn't put my money on it if I were you,' Hal said thinly. 'I caught her turning away a patient who'd had two cardiac arrests and was suffering from chest pains with the diagnosis that he had indigestion!' He raised his eyebrows with wry amusement, and was once again taken aback by the candour and openness of Rosie's face. Here, he felt certain, was a girl who could hide nothing—and who had nothing to hide. He leaned across the table to her. 'So if you see or hear anything that worries you going on in Reception or in the clinic generally, just call me. I'd far rather be safe than sorry. Claire won't mind. She knows herself that she's a total scatterbrain.'

'I'll certainly keep my eyes open,' Rosie promised. 'Tell me, what do you think I ought to wear?'

'In the surgery?' Hal looked surprised. 'Didn't I see you with your old uniform from Highstead just now? Wear that—unless you'd rather not. I expect we could find you a white nylon overall if you'd rather . . .' He couldn't prevent his slightly dubious glance at Rosie's ample bosom. 'I think the patients would prefer uniform, don't you? It gives them more confidence. I sometimes think that they'd have more confidence in me if I wore a uniform!'

'If they lack confidence in you, I'm sure it's only because you're so young.' Rosie heard the flattering words and blushed so violently that she couldn't go on. 'I m-m-mean,' she stammered, 'that older patients seem to prefer older doctors and nurses. It's difficult for them to believe that anyone much younger than themselves can have the experience to look after them properly. I had to spend a long time persuading old Mr Jacobs that I'd bathed a man before.' Realising the import of her words, she came to an embarrassed halt again.

'I'm sure you've bathed dozens of men—and very capably too.' Hal liked it when she blushed. Claire was so different, absolutely shameless. Even when he'd pointed out that she'd taken Rosie to the wrong pub, she'd only said, 'Oh, dear, I hope she's not too uncomfortable.' It had been left to him to come and sort out the mess.

The barman appeared at Rosie's elbow bearing a
large silver tray and a huge plate covered with
freshly-sliced roast beef and a selection of delicious
fresh vegetables. Horse-radish and mustard were
placed on the table, and a bottle of mineral water. 'I
wish I'd decided to order now,' Hal sighed as he
watched her pick up her knife and fork. Rosie felt
uncomfortable at the idea of having to sit and eat in
front of him; she knew she shouldn't. She should be
dieting, living on salads and cottage cheese. But if
he thought that, why had he ordered her a roast
dinner? Maybe because he wanted to make her feel
welcome. The thought pleased her. He wasn't the
ogre she had first thought him.

'I'll leave you to enjoy your dinner in peace.' Hal
rose from his chair and towered over her. 'If you
can get to us for eight-thirty, that would be fine.
Otherwise, come over when you can. The surgery
is down the first road to your right off the main
street. You can't miss it. Sleep well.' With another
friendly wave, he was gone.

He felt angry with Claire as he drove back to his
house—a cottage a mile and a half outside the
village and only a couple of hundred yards from the
water's edge, where his sailing dinghy was kept
moored in the summer.

It wasn't that Claire was a bad person in any way;
he hoped he'd made that perfectly clear to Rosie
Simpson, who'd have every right to feel distressed
at the way she'd been treated. Claire always had the
very best of motives for everything. She'd taken
over the booking of a room to save *him* the trouble.
Everything she did was with the best of intentions.
It was just that sometimes she didn't seem to see

things very clearly—like sending away a seriously ill cardiac patient because she didn't want to bother the overworked GPs . . . He sighed. It was almost as if she was careless with other people's feelings at times. Maybe her divorce from Dick had done that; maybe she just couldn't bring herself to sympathise too closely with anyone. Well, Rosie Simpson was just the opposite. She seemed a caring, careful person, and that was just what was needed to balance Claire's lack of deep interest.

There was no light on in the cottage as he drew up at the front door. Claire must have guessed that he'd feel peeved with her and slipped home. It was only a ten-minute walk down the lane to the flat in a converted barn that he'd found her when she'd called him and begged for help. But she wouldn't be able to stay there cheaply for very much longer, not now that the holiday season was about to get underway. The farmer would want to let it to tourists willing to pay large rents for it . . .

Well, she's not going to move in here, he decided, surveying the empty mugs and plates in his sitting-room. It wasn't just that she was thoughtless enough not to have washed up before she left; he just didn't want to get involved with her again. Hal's eyes caught the photo on the mantelshelf, which was just a black oak beam projecting above the open log fire. In the picture Claire was gazing lovingly at him against a background of his old Oxford college. Why he'd kept it when she'd run off with Dick, he didn't know. But when she'd come to him asking for a job three months ago, he'd found it in the attic and brought it down again. For ages he'd hoped she'd come back. Now she had. So why did he struggle with this feeling of resentment towards her? Why did she manage to annoy him so easily? With a defeated shrug, he picked up her empty plates and took them through to the little kitchen. Well, at least with Nurse Simpson here, he could perhaps share the burden . . .

'This is the reception area.' Mrs Hammond indicated a pleasant, rather olde-worlde waiting area, with chintz cushions on bentwood chairs and a large vase of daffodils on a central table. It was lovely —and quite unlike anything Rosie had met before. 'I brought in the flowers,' Mrs Hammond said proudly. 'We try to make it as pleasant and homely as we can.'

'Oh, it's very nice indeed,' Rosie said warmly.

The senior receptionist led her down the freshly-painted corridor to the surgeries. Although the building itself, once the local Corn Exchange, was old and picturesque, it was very spacious inside and had been sympathetically modernised.

'This is Dr Dickinson's.' She opened the door briefly, and Rosie took in the spacious, airy room, very bright and clean but with chintzy touches that softened the potentially clinical atmosphere. 'And Dr Higgins'.' Another similar room, rather longer and thinner but with the bright glow of a bank of daffodils through the netted window.

'Down here we've got a room for the local health visitor to use, and the community nurse. They're organised from town, of course, but it's useful for them to have a base here for post-natal care and things like that.' Mrs Hammond opened a door on to a huge room divided by pine panelling partitions into a pleasant office area and a simple surgery.

'And now this is the bit that you'll be in most of the time. This will be your surgery.' Rosie almost gasped in amazement. Her room was huge and sunny, with a very businesslike old desk at one end and a treatment area at the other. There were filing cabinets, a treatment couch, and ranges of equipment.

'This is so much more than I expected,' she breathed, taking in the small autoclave, the pneumatic chair, which rose well off the ground to make it easy for her to attend to people's feet, the glass-fronted cupboard full of dressings and bottles. The entire room was warm and flooded with cheerful sunlight. 'It's lovely!'

'Good. I'm glad you approve,' Mrs Hammond smiled. 'I'll bring you in some daffs tomorrow. We've got thousands of them in the garden. Now, through here,' she led Rosie out, through the little waiting area immediately outside the door, to a set of double doors, 'We've got the big room. You'll be told all about the plans for it when you meet the doctors later.'

It was a huge room—fifty feet by thirty at least, Rosie estimated—and open right to the rafters. Long, elegant windows stretched almost to the floor and let in the clear spring light which flooded on to the polished pale oak boards. At one end there was a group of pale oak chairs and a little raised stage.

'It looks like a community hall,' Rosie commented wonderingly. 'What do you use it for?'

'At the moment it's hardly used at all, but we would like to develop it. The only problem is that it's not a good idea having too many people walking through the rest of the centre. Anyway, you'll talk that over later. Now, I'll just show you the common room and then I must get back to Reception.' Mrs Hammond glanced at her watch. 'It's almost half-past-eight. It was very good of you to come in so early.'

'I'm very spoilt up at the Horse and Cart,' Rosie smiled. 'All I had to do was get up. My breakfast was brought on a tray and my bed will be made. It's as good as being on holiday.'

'Happen you won't think it's so much of a holiday once you've met the doctors and talked over what's happening,' Mrs Hammond warned. 'Now, this is the common room. We all use it, doctors and everyone. We put eighty pence each a week into the kitty for milk and coffee, and those who want biscuits bring their own. The money goes into the jar every Tuesday.' She pointed to an earthenware jar on the smart white marble mantelpiece, for this room, as all others in the centre, had obviously been built for gracious living. The open fireplace had been filled in here, and a gas fire installed. It was blazing away and the common room felt cosy.

'You'll need your own mug or cup and saucer, and we try to keep the place clean and tidy.' Mrs Hammond was obviously a bit of a stickler for doing things properly, Rosie thought, and made a mental note. She wondered how Claire Kemp, who didn't seem very bothered about doing anything properly, got on with her.

'I must go now, but you stay and make yourself a cup of coffee. And if you want to go to your room and have a look around, please do. You'll meet the doctors as they come in if you wait here.' Mrs Hammond nodded encouragingly and went out.

What an incredible turn-up for the books, Rosie

thought as she brewed herself a cup of coffee and settled into one of the battered but comfy chairs in the common room. Never in her wildest dreams had she thought places like this existed. The words 'health centre' conjured up visions of either ultra-modern, prefabricated, plasticised blocks in under-developed districts or else gloomy brown-and-cream waiting rooms in dingy converted houses. But this! It was huge and welcoming and in every way delightful.

After her good night's sleep in the soft bed at the Horse and Cart she had woken with enthusiasm for the new day, but now she could scarcely wait to get going. What would the lunchtime meeting with the doctors bring? Would she be able to cope with their ideas and demands? Nothing would stop her!

'Aha – you must be our new nurse. Pleased to meet you.' An attractive man in early middle age disturbed her thoughts as he came into the room. 'I'm Philip Higgins.' He held out his hand welcomingly.

'And I'm Rosie Simpson,' Rosie said, and her optimism and excitement lent a glow to her cheeks and a shine to her eyes that distracted from her unfashionably ripe figure.

'We're very pleased that you agreed to come and give us a hand here. I'm sure you'll be very happy. I think,' he referred to an expensive-looking watch, 'that I'd better get into my surgery now. I'll have the Monday morning queue forming. If we get anyone suitable for you to see, will you take them this morning? Nothing like plunging in at the deep end!'

'I hadn't really . . . I don't know where . . . Oh, all right!' Keyed up by his automatic assumption that she could cope with anything he sent her, Rosie assented with a shy smile. To have someone express such faith in her was a compliment, and she could only accept it gracefully.

Philip led her out of the common room and turned her in the right direction for her own surgery —for she'd totally lost her bearings on Mrs Hammond's guided tour. 'I'll only send you people you'll have no trouble with,' he promised. 'Then when you've had time to settle in and find your way around, we'll see what you want to do.' His grin, surprisingly impish for a man in his forties, or so Rosie guessed him to be, was catching, and she found herself returning it in kind.

'I'll call you if I have any problems,' she promised.

'Yes, and ask Mrs Hammond if you can't find anything. She's the person who really runs this place.' With a cheerful wave, he made his way back to his own surgery.

Inside her room, Rosie tried to prepare for any eventualities that might come her way during the morning. She opened the cupboards and found supplies of dressings and equipment. There was an allergy kit in one cupboard, full of little bottles and forms. The desk contained more forms. Leafing through them, the most important seemed to be that on which she should record the treatment given to any patient. Maybe I should keep a list of materials I use, too, she decided, and drew up a sheet on which to enter things that would need to be reordered. In her bag she had a couple of general textbooks, which she took out and hid carefully in the drawer. Something that she hadn't had to deal with for years *might* just come in, and then a reference might be handy. But she sincerely hoped that she wouldn't need it. Just as she was putting on one of the disposable plastic aprons she'd found stored in their packets, there came a knock on the door.

'Come in,' Rosie called, feeling suddenly nervous at the prospect of her first patient. There was a silence; the door didn't open. Cautiously, just in case she was hearing things, Rosie opened it. A defiant elderly face scrutinised her from the hallway.

'I thought you weren't in,' the old man said shortly.

'Oh, but I am,' Rosie replied diplomatically.

'Eh? What's that you say, lass? You'll have to speak up a bit—I'm a mite deaf.' And so saying, he shuffled past her and into the surgery. 'Yon woman on reception desk said as I have to see you and not Dr Higgins. That's right, is it?'

'Yes, it is,' Rosie shouted. 'Can I take a few details, Mr . . . ?'

He made himself comfortable on the chair and told her a few details. She filled in her form studiously and hoped, since no one had seen fit to tell her what to do, that it was all right. 'Now, what's wrong, Mr Walters?' Talking at such volume had begun to make her throat ache already. She'd forgotten just how wearisome it could be, dealing with elderly patients.

'I've got a nasty boil, lass. On me shoulder. I was going to get the doctor to lance it. Can you do that?' His look suggested that he doubted her capabilities, but he was obviously reassured by her appearance, because as she helped him off with his coat, woolly and vest and took a look at the troublesome boil he said, 'I were expecting a chit of a young thing, but you look as if you know what you're doing.'

'Oh yes, I've done this sort of thing before,' Rosie soothed him. Goodness yes, she'd lanced a few boils in her time. And what luck that her first case was one which she could cope with so easily.

Covering her patient with a blanket as he lay on the couch, so that he didn't get cold, she prepared a tray—a scalpel, antibacterial lotion and a dressing. 'Right,' she said, swabbing the area firmly, 'brace yourself, Mr Walters, here we go.' Ten minutes later, with his shoulder well-padded, the old gentleman made his way out.

'Your next patient's here, Nurse,' he called loudly from the hall. 'I'll see you next time, eh?'

Rosie beamed and waved him off before bringing in the next patient. 'Dr Higgins wants you to do some allergy tests. Here's the card.' The young woman who handed the allergy form to Rosie was very smart and rather cold in her manner. She wore a fitted tweed suit with stylish but sensible brown brogues and thick tights. Rosie couldn't help feeling that the girl looked old before her time—but then, that was the way that wealthy country folk preferred to look, she knew from her time in Devon. And she wasn't, she reminded herself, in London now, with a boutique on every street corner.

'Come in and sit down. Is there anything that you suspect you might be allergic to?' Rosie asked, moving over to the cupboard to withdraw the allergy set.

'I rather thought that it was your job to find that

out,' came the cool reply. 'If I knew what I was allergic to . . .'

'It's just that it saves time and discomfort for you,' Rosie interrupted quickly, before the patient could get carried away. 'Every substance that I test you for will require a scratch on your forearm. If you suspect, for example, that you might be allergic to animal hair or certain types of grass or pollen.'

'How would I know about things like that?' the girl asked poutingly.

'Because you might have noticed that you're better or worse at certain times of the year. Or that you feel particularly ill after stroking dogs or cats,' Rosie explained patiently. Sometimes people could be so dense!

'I think you'd better try them all,' was the patient's only response.

'Very well, please roll your sleeves up and place your arms on the table, hands up.' Deciding that in this case it was best to be strictly professional, Rosie set out her bottles and the disposable pricker. 'Now, I'm just going to mark your forearms with code in Biro, so that we can remember what went where.'

The girl looked aghast but said nothing as Rosie counted the bottles and then, working at even gaps of about an inch and a half, scrawled the codes of each of the bottles on her arm. The blue Biro looked messy against her very white skin. The next step was to note on a separate sheet of paper the order in which the concentrated extracts were applied to the skin. Then Rosie broke the surface of the skin very gently with the emery-board style pricker. 'And now we apply the extracts.' A single drop of each was applied to the roughened skin, and gradually it dried.

'You can roll your sleeves down now and wait ten minutes outside, please. Don't let the fabric of your blouse touch the skin. It might create a reaction.'

'Why did you have to scrape me like that?' the girl asked, rolling down her sleeves. 'I hope it won't take long to heal. I've got a party at the end of the week and I wanted to wear short sleeves.'

'If you get a bad reaction to one of them you might have to find a dress with long sleeves. We roughen the skin so that the extract takes effect quickly. Otherwise you might have to wait hours before anything happened. Or it might not respond at all.'

Still looking sceptical, the girl went out. There was no one else waiting for attention, so Rosie set about clearing up. If this was the kind of problem she was going to get, she knew for certain that she was going to enjoy this job very much. It was the kind of basic stuff that students everywhere are taught, and yet, strangely, it was some of the most satisfying. You could spend days working with people on wards and see little improvement in them; and they didn't even thank you for your attention at times. But with this sort of thing, you were actually able to give some help or relief. And there was none of the soul-destroying menial work that prevented nurses from being thought of as true professionals—the washing and the feeding. She felt positively happy as she washed her hands and put more papers into plastic folders so that she could see them easily.

Another loud knock on the door made her shout, 'Come in.' And then, fearing that it might be another deaf patient, she went to open it. It flew open in her face.

Hal Dickinson entered the room and stared in disbelief. 'Who told you to open shop?' he asked, taking in the changes that had already overcome the rather stark and empty surgery—the cupboard doors open, the dressing packet on the preparation unit, the stainless steel dishes off their shelves.

'Dr Higgins. He's sent me a couple of patients, too, so that I could get started. Why, is there a problem?'

Hal looked at her, cheeks rosy and eyes sparkling with enjoyment. Nurse Simpson was in her element. Nurse Simpson was at large—and doing very well, by the looks of things. 'No,' he said simply. 'It's just that I haven't been through the paperwork with you yet. You weren't supposed to start anything until after our meeting this afternoon.' He grinned. 'I'm not going to stop you if you're happy. Keep up the good work, Nurse!'

CHAPTER FOUR

A GLOW of pleasure shot through Rosie, leaving her feeling weak and flushed and quite inexplicably like turning a somersault—though that was out of the question. And yet even as she felt herself respond to Hal's encouragement, cautionary warnings came creeping into her head. Remember what had happened over Giles Levete; a single act of encouragement, a few kind words from him, and she had fancied herself head-over-heels in love. Totally, disastrously infatuated—that was what she had been. She could see quite clearly now, of course, but at the time she had believed herself truly in love with the man. And all sorts of things had happened.

But they brought you here . . . A little voice, tempting her to imagine things that could never come true, whispered in her ear. Perhaps it's fate; perhaps Giles Levete came along so that you could jack in your job and meet Hal Dickinson. Perhaps *he's* the man . . .

Rosie clattered the receiver in the sink, dipped the scalpel in fluid and put both stainless steel items in the steriliser, trying to drown that treacherous voice and its ideas. Why could she never stop fantasising that one day a gorgeous man would come along and fall in love with her—when no self-respecting man would want to get involved with a plump, ungainly nurse! Stop living in a dream world, Rosie, she lectured herself. The kind of man who's going to take any romantic interest in

you is likely to be the sort of man you wouldn't want
around . . .

'Excuse me. The time's up. Do you want to have
a look at my arm? And Dr Dickinson's sent down
another patient.' The smart young woman had
crept into the room without Rosie noticing, and she
jumped at her voice.'Oh yes. Let's see what we've
got.' The girl rolled up her sleeves again. Three red
blotches glowed violently against the pale skin and
the blue Biro marks. 'Do they itch badly?' Rosie
asked as she checked the chart and the marks to see
what they were.

'They're very itchy. Can you do something about
them?'

'We can give you a dab of antihistamine cream.
That should calm them,' Rosie said absent-
mindedly. 'Well, you're allergic to animal fur, dust
mites and the pollen of the elder family of trees. Do
you have animals at home?'

The girl looked annoyed. 'Yes, dogs—and
horses. I ride nearly every day. Does this mean I'm
going to have to give it up? And what about dust? I
wouldn't have said that my house was particularly
dusty,' she sniffed.

'I think the best thing in this case, bearing in
mind that we can't ask you to give up your animals
all of a sudden, is to put you on a course of
immunising injections that will gradually build you
resistance to the allergies. Would you be able to
pop in once a week for ten or twelve weeks?' Rosie
wondered if she had the authority to write a prescription for something like this, and decided that
she didn't. She'd have to send the girl back to Dr
Higgins with a note. She filled in the allergy card
that the girl had arrived with.

'It's a terrible nuisance,' protested the patient, who was called Veronica Reitz. 'Isn't there anything else?'

'You can have antihistamine tablets which will help, but they may make you very sleepy. And anyway, if this allergic reaction is going to go on indefinitely, without proper treatment you'd have to stay on the tablets. The injections really are the best thing.' As she spoke, Rosie tipped some surgical spirit onto a pad of cotton wool and did her best to clean away the Biro marks. Then she dabbed cortisone cream on the worst affected patch tests. 'If you want to think about it, please feel free. I'll keep the allergy test card here, just in case you want to come back.'

'No, it's best to get it over and done with,' the girl admitted grouchily. 'What do you want me to do?'

'So, you could cope with routine breast examinations and the odd smear test and internal, if we had a lady who would prefer it with a nurse. All small wounds and dressings, the allergies—might be a good idea if we had an allergies clinic as they're becoming so much more fashionable—pregnancy testing, some pre- and post-natal work . . .' Hal looked up from the list he was compiling. 'Tell me, Nurse Simpson, is there anything you *can't* do?'

Across the table from him in the common room, where they were holding a post-lunch meeting to sort out what she would do in the future, Rosie blushed violently. 'I see from Nurse Simpson's personal details that she did two years working in the Casualty department of a London hospital—so there's probably not a lot she can't do,' Mrs Hammond chipped in.

'Praise indeed from Mrs Hammond, Rosie, my dear,' Dr Higgins smiled, draining the last of his coffee. Rosie liked him. He was such an encouraging person, so positive. Not like Hal Dickinson who, though pleasant these days, always managed to suggest just a touch of amusement. But then Rosie thought dryly, he's seen me at my worst —half-asleep and smothered in jam! He has every right to be sceptical about my abilities. Strangely, though, it was he who seemed most determined to use her as much as possible in the health centre.

'There are a couple of my pet projects that I'd like you to have a think about Rosie.' So, he'd been challenged by Dr Higgins' familiarity to drop her title, had he?

'I want to set up a course of once-weekly classes for those coming up to retirement, to show them how to stay fit and healthy and prepare them for having time on their hands. We find that so many of them discover that retirement is not quite what they'd hoped for. As a side-line to that, I'm hoping that someone from the community centre will start a lunch club or something in the big hall.' Hal stared Rosie in the eye. 'How would you feel about exercise classes?'

He knew it would embarrass her. It was rather like asking a heavy smoker what he thought about lung cancer, or a vegetarian about meat. Rosie looked at the table for a few seconds.

'I don't quite know what you mean,' she admitted at last.

'I want to establish a pensioners' exercise class—nothing strenuous, just a few bends and stretches. Think you could get that organised? We don't want anything too exotic, and a qualified

person ought to run it, just in case.' Those navy
eyes seemed to penetrate right to the back of her
mind. 'It might do you good, too,' he said merci-
lessly, not letting her off the hook for a moment.

'Ah, and I think a class for the pregnant mums
might be a good idea, too, while we're at it,' Dr
Higgins added. 'Some breathing exercises, a few
simple moves to keep their muscle tone up and
some advice on how to strengthen the pelvic floor
—that kind of thing. Nothing complicated.'

Rosie nodded and set it down in her notebook.
At the rate things were going, she'd be practically
running the place before long! However had they
coped without a nurse before?

'Now, we've agreed that you're to take over
routine inoculations, so I'll transfer all the relevant
paperwork into your office,' Hal noted. 'And you
understand our system—the forms and everything?'

'Oh yes—nothing like as complicated as the
hospital forms,' Rosie said quickly and honestly.
Sometimes nursing could be badly hampered by
bureaucracy.

'And you won't mind too much if we channel
some of our regulars who only come for a chat in
your direction, so that they don't occupy Hal and
Philip's time?' asked Claire, who had been loung-
ing nonchalantly back in her seat on the other side
of Dr Higgins. 'I mean, maybe we could send you
Minny and Miss Loadesley—and then if you think
that they really *do* have anything wrong with them,
you can refer them to the doctors.'

'Well,' Rosie said as tactfully as she could, 'I'm
going to be fairly busy myself, so I don't really want
all the problem patients.'

'And quite right too. Rosie's a professional, doing a full time job. You're not to lumber her with our difficult characters just to make your own life easier, Claire. It's your job to cope with them and discourage them from using this place like the local corner shop. Rosie's going to be busy here. I won't have you thinking of her as some sort of soft option.' Hal saw Claire's eyes widen with shock, but he couldn't retract the hard words, and nor did he want to. Claire wasn't really cut out for dealing with the people who came in to use the health centre. She would have been fine as receptionist in some smart clinic, but here she didn't seem to know what to say to the elderly patients or the young mums. Sometimes he'd seen her confusion when something she'd said with the best of intentions, trying to be friendly, had been taken the wrong way. And how could he ask her to keep her entire attention on the job when he knew what she'd been through these past few months? Exasperation, sympathy, and some deep resistance seemed to twist within him when he thought of her.

'Now, you'll want to go and have a look at the flat, I expect,' Mrs Hammond said, breaking the uncomfortable silence that had overtaken them. 'I'm afraid I've got to pop off, but I'm sure . . .'

'I'll show you around up there,' Philip Higgins ventured, patting Rosie's hand vigorously—a bit too vigorously for her liking. 'It'll give us a few minutes to get to know each other better.'

'No, you'd better go off on your rounds. I know you said you'd go over to the school at Hayfield this afternoon.' Why he had interrupted, Hal didn't know. The last thing he wanted to do was to show his gauche new nurse over the flat she would eventually occupy—if it suited her. It wasn't as if he hadn't enough to do . . .

Rosie sensed his impatience and wondered why he'd put his foot down so firmly against Dr Higgins showing her around. In fact she was beginning to feel distinctly uncomfortable. First Hal had been rude to Claire Kemp and now he'd rebuffed Philip Higgins. It wouldn't exactly help her case and make her settling-in period easy if the two of them decided that she was out to cause trouble. 'There's no need, honestly,' she murmured, pulling her chair away from the table and trying to put an end to the difficult atmosphere. 'I can wait until it's more convenient.'

'It's perfectly convenient.' Hal gritted his teeth. 'I wouldn't have offered to take you up there if it wasn't.'

He was just as he had been that first day she had met him down in Devon, she thought with a start —vaguely polite but with disdain and coldness seeping through the façade of helpfulness. Why did he have to change so suddenly? Why couldn't he be as he had been the other night at the hotel or this morning in the surgery? When he'd smiled at her like that, or said those encouraging words, she could almost believe that he liked her. But now she felt as she had that morning after he'd woken her in his father's room; a nuisance, not to be trusted, a time-wasting, unlovable lump.

Claire and Philip Higgins brushed past as they went to the door, both of them stiff and silent. Mrs Hammond was putting on her coat and looking for her shopping basket. 'Come on then, let's get it over with.' Hal ushered a silent Rosie through the door and out of the main entrance of the clinic. She felt as if she was some tedious task to be got over quickly; like the cabbage on the plate, to be eaten first so that he might enjoy something more choice later.

'Honestly, Dr Dickinson,' she protested as he steered her with gestures and a firm step to the side of the building and down a short passage to where another white-painted door had been knocked into the place, 'there's no need.'

'It's all right.' He turned to her as he tried to find the right key for the Yale lock. 'I'm sorry, Rosie, it's not you I'm angry with. It's myself for behaving so badly towards poor Claire and Philip. Don't take anything personally, will you?' And his smile was genuine—the sort he had only rewarded her with once or twice before and which made her insides quake with sheer feminine pleasure at his male good looks.

The door opened at last, revealing a small hallway with meters in a cupboard and an elegant sweep of mahogany banisters and handrail. 'This entrance was knocked through a few years ago,' Hal explained, shutting the door behind them. It was almost dark and when he went to turn on the light switch by the door nothing happened. 'They must be still finishing the electrics,' he said simply. 'I'll go up first. Careful where you tread, there are probably boards still up.'

His loping stride took him up the stairs well ahead of Rosie, who found herself panting slightly as she reached the top. But it wasn't just the exertion of the stairs that made her heart beat faster. It was the sight of him in front of her, waiting at the top of the stairs with a boyish grin on his face. 'You seem to have liked everything you've seen so far, Nurse Simpson, so I hope you won't be disappointed.' He opened a door off the landing, and Rosie found herself looking into a small flat. It had been built in the eaves of the old place and had sloping ceilings that reflected the shape of the roof. Nevertheless, the sitting-room, which they had entered, was a good size and had a splendid view of the back garden. Rosie couldn't keep the smile of pleasure from her face.

'Oh, it's lovely!' she exclaimed, and even with some of the floorboards up and a patch of plaster missing from one of the walls where a radiator had been put in, it was. She could just imagine it decorated with a few simple furnishings and her own bits and pieces collected over the years of her flat-shares and nurses' homes.

'Kitchen.' Hal opened another door off the landing to reveal a kitchen just large enough to take a table to eat at, a few newly-installed worktops and a shiny sink-unit. 'Nothing very glamorous, I'm afraid,' he smiled apologetically. 'We couldn't stretch to pine and parquet, but it should be sufficient for the time being—especially if you've been living in a nurses' home recently.'

'I was sharing a flat, actually, but it wasn't nearly as nice as this.' Rosie's shyness almost held her back, but she said coyly, 'Anyway, what do you know about nurses' homes?'

Hal coughed and looked embarrassed for a moment. 'I had what some might call a misspent youth,' he replied with a twinkle in his eye. 'I seemed to spend nearly all my time as a medical student either trying to break into them after hours or out of them before I could be discovered. Claire hated them so much that she used to . . .'

His smile faded as he saw Rosie blush, and he led
the way to the bathroom, which was pristine all-
white, rather like a hospital, and a bedroom with a
couple of fitted cupboards. Rosie took it all in as
through a mist. His hint about a relationship between himself and Claire, so long suspected but
never really made clear, had hit her with full force.
Suddenly the balloon of happiness that seemed to
have been welling in her for so much of the day
began to deflate. Hal Dickinson and Claire Kemp
had been contemporaries; boy and girl-friend.
Claire had been, a nurse. She'd been training,
anyway, that much was clear.

Just when she'd thought that the ice was beginning to break, that they were getting somewhere,
Rosie realised with shock just how little she knew
of the man standing before her. And she admitted
with shame to herself that already she was beginning to weave silly little daydreams around him
—to imagine things that could simply never happen. And all because he'd been kind to her once or
twice. He was just a kind man, once one got
through that grouchy exterior, she lectured herself
as she gazed around the bedroom and wandered
automatically over to take a look at the interior of
the cupboards. She could be happy here, in this
little flat with these friendly people around. She
would not blow it this time by getting involved in
any way.

'Well, what do you think? Will it do?' Sensing
her preoccupation, Hal stood back.

'Oh yes, it's perfect. Far nicer than I deserve.'
Rosie couldn't bear to look him in the eye, fearful
that she might give away her deepest thoughts and
make him laugh at her presumption, as had

happened in the past when some handsome, inaccessible young man had discovered that she held a torch for him.

'What nonsense, Rosie!' Hal laughed, but not unkindly. 'I wish that I could offer the best for the best, but unfortunately this was all we could manage. We'll have it carpeted for you in something functional and you can find a sofa and a bed and a cooker—we'll pick up the bill for those. Do you have any furniture of your own?'

'Not much, but a few bits and pieces. It'll be lovely to have a proper home for once, not just a room in a flat.' Yes, she thought to herself, it would be wonderful to belong to this community, to have her own place here. She would do nothing to jeopardise it.

'Good, it will be nice having someone to live on the premises—it will bring some real life back into the old place.' Hal perched nonchalantly on one of the wide windowsills. 'Seriously, do you think you're going to be happy here?'

'Yes, I don't see how I couldn't be.' Rosie fumbled with a piece of paper she'd found in her uniform pocket and tried to ignore his eyes piercing her and her embarrassment at being so big and ungainly and not worth looking at. 'You've been so nice—I mean you've all been so nice . . .' she faltered.

'Well, I like to get the best out of my staff. You see, I don't see general practice as being just a job. I want this place to become a centre for community life. That's why I've had it done up in such an informal way, why we don't have a proper waiting room and all that.' He looked troubled for a moment, running his long fingers against the glass and looking out over the street below.

'I know Philip thinks I'm something of a crank. He'd like us to keep our mystique, have pokey little rooms full of impressive-looking books and shiny equipment. But I think that a surgery should be a place that people can relax in and feel at home in. I'd like to think that they can come and talk to us here *before* they feel ill. That's why I want to have the old folks' meetings in the hall downstairs and things going on in the afternoons when the surgeries are over. I think that we GPs should be leading the way, showing people how they can look after themselves, keeping them active, that sort of thing. Not just patching them up when their bodies give them trouble.'

There was a dark glow in his eyes as he turned back, and Rosie felt a shudder of excitement run through her. It all sounded so exciting when he talked like that. He gave a sense of purpose to the venture. Yes, how much better if GPs could help prevent illness and problems just as much as cure them! In his face she could see the enthusiasm and energy of a truly motivated man. She'd seen it burn in the eyes of some of Highstead's top surgeons, men whose dedication to their professions had saved hundreds of lives and kept them going when those around them had dropped. Charismatic, strong men.

'You're very quiet. Perhaps you think I'm a crank too.' His statement held the hint of a question.

'Oh no! I think that what you say is right. Of course, it's the most difficult thing to do,' she admitted guardedly. 'People don't always behave in a very convenient fashion. They tend to want to talk for hours about their problems, and never when you've got the time to spare. And some of them you can't help no matter what you do. But it would be nice to feel that you were a central part of the community, instead of just somewhere people went when they didn't feel well.'

'Another convert!' Hal grinned, and his navy eyes sparkled. 'Philip will be hopping mad when he finds that there are three of us on the premises.'

'Who's the other one?' Rosie asked nervously, expecting to hear Claire's name rising from his lips. Somehow the fact that Claire, too, believed in these ideals flattened them. It would be so nice to think that there was something, just one little thing, that she could share with Hal Dickinson.

'Mrs Hammond of course. She's wonderful in Reception, very calming and not at all the old dragon. She believes as I do—that you can't just process people as if you were running a production line. That's why I decided to ask you to come, in fact.' His voice was low and friendly. He couldn't be having her on, Rosie decided quickly.

'Me?' she stuttered. 'I don't think you were too impressed by my nursing the first time you saw me.'

'You're not intimidating. You're a good nurse —I checked that out with someone at Highstead who I trained with. Oh yes, I did my homework,' he laughed at her astounded face. 'And I should say, Nurse Simpson, that I heard nothing but good, so that should boost your confidence. And anyway, I liked the way you looked after my father, even if you didn't know the latest thoughts about finger lacerations. You look dependable and comfort-able, and that's what counts here. You've already won some firm supporters among the patients, so I know that I was right.'

'Thank you,' Rosie said automatically, yet she didn't know whether she *did* thank him or not. Comfortable; dependable; not intimidating . . . It didn't add up to much, did it? It really just meant that she was a solid workhorse who probably wouldn't go getting herself into trouble or running off to get married. How could he say such a thing and imagine she would take it as a compliment?

Hal uncrossed his long legs and rose from the windowsill. He was so attractive that Rosie couldn't help watching him; so vital, even in that mundane movement, that she felt her senses stir within her. And yet she mustn't, she knew, get involved, because it would not only make her unhappy, it would also ruin her future here. And that future could be very rewarding and interesting indeed, she could feel it in her bones. How could it not be interesting with a man like Hal around?

'We'd better go back down now,' he said casually as he led her out and back down the stairs. 'I've got a case conference and then some visits. Why don't you sit down and start some serious planning for these meetings we're going to hold in the hall?' And with a brief pat on the back to reassure her, a pat that sent the blood racing through her veins as if it had been a passionate kiss, he turned down the corridor to his own office.

CHAPTER FIVE

'Now don't force it, especially if you've got a bad back, but just bend as far as you comfortably can . . .' Rosie, pink-faced and beginning to feel the exertion of these supposedly mild exercises that had been worked out by a friendly physiotherapist at Woodbridge Hospital, demonstrated the bend. Ouch! She could feel her plump shoulders aching and the backs of her knees tugging. Well, if she could do it, so could most of her class of retired people.

'Now bounce very gently while you're in that position, and you should be able to feel the muscles tightening each time. Keep this up and you should be able to stay supple.' She repeated the cheery words that the physio had expressed as she'd shown Rosie the routine in the confines of the hospital work-out room. 'Don't overdo it, Mrs Spivey. Just gently at first. Keep your legs straight, Mrs English. That's right!'

The tape of rhythmic music that played quietly in the background kept everyone in time, and despite the fact that this was the first meeting of the Over Sixties club, it all looked surprisingly well-organised and professional, with twenty-two elderly backs bent more or less supply and bouncing in time to the music. 'Now, straighten up and lift your arms . .'

There were one or two sighs of relief and Mrs English, with an apologetic wave, went to sit down at the side of the room to watch the proceedings, but everyone seemed very good-humoured. Rosie, in her specially-purchased grey track suit and sweatshirt, knew she looked a sight, but she'd decided that it was no good trying to get people's confidence and encourage them to keep fit if she half-heartedly did the exercises in her uniform with its seams straining. No, she'd have to do it properly, and after some initial embarrassment that one so obviously unfit should be teaching fitness classes, everyone had had a laugh and settled down to the session.

'If you can do it, my dear,' someone had said good-naturedly, 'then I'm willing to give it a go. Maybe it'll do us all some good.'

Rosie was in the middle of showing them how to do some spine-stretching exercises, useful for those with bad backs, when she sensed the door behind her opening. Nervously she turned around, suddenly self-conscious. These older people seemed able to accept her as she was, but Claire Kemp had expressed a couple of slightly snide remarks about people practising what they preached, implying that it was wrong for Rosie to be involved with fitness teaching. 'I could do it,' she'd protested to Hal and Philip at one of their meetings, but Hal had met her comment with a cool,

'It's better that a trained nurse does it, just in case of accidents,' and that had been that. Maybe, Rosie frowned, Claire had come along to gloat. And gloat she would, having seen Nurse Simpson's ample derriere in unflattering track pants . . .

'Hallo, everything okay?' Hal smiled through the six-inch opening in the door, taking in the sight before him. Not just Rosie's over-generous bottom but twenty more glowing faces.

'Yes, thank you.' Pinker than ever, Rosie held up the proceedings and waited for him to go and Hal, realising that she was too shy to go on in front of him, nodded encouragingly and shut the door, a faint grin on his face. It *was* funny to see such an amply-built girl leading a work-out, but there was admiration and more in his smile. He had begun to realise just how painfully shy she was, particularly with him, and with other men. And he'd also begun to realise what a godsend she was to the place. Since she'd arrived, the health centre had taken on the dimension he had felt was lacking, yet which he hadn't had time to provide himself. Three weeks, was it? And already she'd arranged not only this weekly keep-fit and social club for the older citizens of Clayburgh, but she'd also got the regular ante-natal and mother's club off the ground. And all this on top of running her own little surgery and dealing with her own patients. He would do nothing to hurt her or offend her, Hal decided, walking back to his own surgery. She might not be the trim *femme fatale* he'd like to be seen around with, or the confident leader he would have liked. But who ever would have thought, after their first, inauspicious meeting, that she could be taking all this on, and with such self-deprecating success?

Back in the hall Rosie resumed the stretches and bends. Beads of perspiration began to shine on her forehead, and those of some of her less fit charges. It was quite a relief to wind down with some relaxing exercises on the floor. 'Now we're all going to practise some breathing exercises,' she announced.

'What, you mean we haven't been breathing

through all that lot?' gasped some wit, and there
was a round of laughter.

'No!' Rosie joined in the merriment. 'But we can
teach ourselves to relax by breathing properly, and
we can also ensure that our lungs get the proper
exercise they need.' And for another ten minutes
she showed them all how to breathe deeply from
the diaphragm and how to slowly relax themselves
into an almost sleep-like state. It was lovely, lying
on the polished wood floor of the warm room on a
lovely sunny spring day, so exercised and relaxed
that the world seemed a million miles away, Rosie
thought as she watched the second hand of the
clock go round. Five minutes, that was all she
would give them . . .

'Here, I think Mr Benson's a bit too relaxed,'
came an amused voice from the back of the hall.
'He's snoring!'

'Wake him up, someone, and we'll have some
tea,' Rosie laughed, and slowly, reluctantly, everyone began to get to their feet. There were a few
grumbles about stiffness, but generally everyone
seemed to have enjoyed the session.

'We ought to start training for marathon running,' someone suggested, and Rosie wondered
with panic if he was only joking, because *she'd*
certainly never be able to do that.

'Dr Dickinson could take us all out for a jog. I see
him go past the cottage most mornings with that
receptionist from here,' added someone else.

'I don't suppose they want any company,' Mrs
Spivey said pointedly, with what used to be known
as an old-fashioned look.

'I'll go and warn the ladies that we're ready for
some tea,' Rosie murmured hurriedly, and dashed

to the kitchen a few yards down from the hall, where a couple of WRVS volunteers had been preparing tea. Also waiting was Mr Laurence, a retired bank manager from one of the surrounding villages, who had agreed to give a short talk about money and investments and who had agreed to come every month or so to the meetings to provide confidential advice on people's financial problems. He smiled as Rosie entered.

'Are they all ready for my boring lecture?' he asked genially. 'After all that exercise I expect they'll fall asleep.'

'They're actually very interested to hear what you've got to say,' Rosie said firmly. 'Quite a few of them have already told me that they want to talk to you about their little investments and their pensions.'

After a few more minutes spent chatting to Mr Laurence she said goodbye and furtively, still in her track suit, left the health centre and ran down the side passage to her own front door.

Three weeks had seen some change in the flat, too. Basic beige carpeting had been laid and Rosie had taken an afternoon off to go into Ipswich and find herself a comfy sofa, a cooker, fridge and one or two other necessities. Her trunk had arrived from Devon and been collected by Hal from the station, and so already the newness of the place had been tempered by her photos, her utensils in the kitchen and a few ornaments and knick-knacks collected during her life in London. Still, it didn't seem much, she thought ruefully as she surveyed the scene. Other people her age had houses full of junk and possessions. But then, she reprimanded herself, if she'd wanted those things she should never have become a nurse, because nurses could never aspire to wealth. And since being a nurse was all she'd ever really wanted and since, right at this moment, being a nurse was all she could imagine herself being, she would just have to be content.

She looked at the clock on the mantelpiece. Four-twenty. She could have a bath and wash her hair and then have some tea, before going down for the five-thirty surgery and more problems that needed to be treated or solved . . .

Hal ushered the health visitor to the door of the centre, saw her into her car and then turned back towards his office. It was ridiculous to go home at this time; he'd no sooner have got there than it would be time to come back. Even so, he could do with a cup of tea and a few minutes' relaxation before starting the evening surgery. Laughter from the main hall halted him for a moment and he turned in that direction, wondering whether Rosie would still be there. She wasn't, but Mr Laurence, the rather dour-looking bank manager, was keeping everyone splendidly entertained with his stories of banking life while tea was served. Hal accepted a cup from one of the volunteers and sat down on a chair at the back of the hall to listen. Soon the bank manager's stories turned from anecdotes to sound advice about what to do with small investments. He seemed to lay a great deal of emphasis on people claiming their rightful benefits, too, and Hal smiled to himself. He hoped Mr Packer and the others like him were listening. They refused all sorts of help to which they were perfectly entitled because they thought it was all in the way of despised charity.

Maybe the bank manager's admission that he accepted rate rebates and free prescriptions would teach them a lesson or two. After all, how could a GP expect to treat people for bronchitis if each winter his patients lived in ice boxes and spent their last pennies eking out the rates bill?

He said as much to Mr Laurence after the gentleman had left the platform to polite applause.

'Oh, that was your nurse's doing.' Mr Laurence smilingly shook his head. 'I wouldn't have thought of it, but she asked me to mention it. It seems that she feels the way you do—that sometimes people are their own worst enemies.'

'I'd certainly agree with that,' Hal said with amused firmness. In the hall Mrs English had lifted the lid of the piano so, wishing everyone well, Hal beat a hasty retreat. His intention was to go back to his office, but somehow his feet didn't seem inclined to take him in that direction. Knowing where he really wanted to go, even if he knew that it was a mistake, he found himself knocking on Rosie's door.

'Hallo.' She stood self-consciously in the doorway, still pink from her exertion and her warm bath, and swathed in a big print smock.

'Hallo.' For only the third or fourth time in his life, Hal found himself short of words. An uneasy sensation began to crawl up his spine as he remembered those other times. They'd all of them been with women; women he'd been attached to, whether he'd known it at the time or not. And he could surely never imagine himself attached to Nurse Simpson . . . Not Nurse Simpson! 'I'm afraid that I'm playing truant from work,' he said lamely, wondering whether he ought to put his foot in the door before she slammed it on him. 'I wondered if you would make me a cup of tea while I tell you how clever you've been.'

Had he been drinking? Rosie wondered for a moment, looking into those navy eyes and seeing a strange glint in their depths. 'There's plenty of tea in the common room,' she said clumsily. 'Not that I don't mean you're not welcome, but there's no need to think you've got to . . .'

'I didn't think I'd *got* to do anything,' Hal said sharply, and entered the hall. 'I just thought I'd come and say well done for today's effort, particularly for your bright idea of getting Mr Laurence to speak to everyone.'

Rosie was suddenly aware of his physicality, his presence, which had so impressed her on their first meeting. Close-to he was straight and strong and muscular in a slim fashion. He seemed to glow with a special masculine vitality that made her insides compress and her mind thud at the same time, which was all so confusing. She put one hand to her forehead. 'Go up, please.' Half of her objected to the way he'd muscled in demanding refreshment and full of bland compliments. The other half merely rejoiced that he *had* come. But what chance would she have of ignoring him as a man if he insisted on making himself a social visitor, she chided as she filled the kettle and put some chocolate biscuits on a plate.

'Your exercise class went well by the look of it—no one carried out on a stretcher, though maybe we'll have a strain or two to deal with this evening,' Hal smiled as Rosie came into the sitting-room with the tray. She looked so innocent, so naive. He had an odd sensation of wanting to look after her, protect her from anything nasty—though why he should begin to feel paternal about her he didn't know, he thought grimly.

'There were no complaints, anyway,' Rosie agreed, pouring him a good strong cuppa, just like she had a hundred doctors over the years. There was a silence. She forced herself to go on. 'You said that the talk went down well,' she faltered.

'Oh yes—they'll all be off to Woodbridge or even Ipswich tomorrow in the search for higher rates of interest. The National Savings Bank won't know what's hit it when it opens tomorrow!' Hal chuckled appreciatively and Rosie smiled. 'I thought it was a good idea of yours to ask Mr Laurence to do his bit to promote the uptake of benefits.'

'Actually, I've been thinking,' Rosie said swiftly. 'I think we can go one better. I think we could get a speaker from the DHSS or the Citizen's Advice Bureau or somewhere to give a whole talk about benefits. It wouldn't just be for the old folk, it would be useful for everyone. We ought to hold it one evening, so that everyone could make sure that they're claiming what they're entitled to. In these country areas with low wages people often don't realise they could get a bit of extra help . . .' She tailed off. She didn't want to suggest to Hal that his patients were all poor or ill-informed, but it was true that a rural area could be just as depressed in its way as a town. And somehow in London people seemed more aware of their entitlements.

'I've had another idea, too. It was something that Mrs Loach said, about being mugged one night in Woodbridge . . .'

'Mugged in Woodbridge!' Hal let out a roar of laughter. 'Rosie, you're just down from the bright lights of the city I know, but honestly, such things don't go on down here. Mrs Loach was approached by a youth who asked rather aggressively for a pound for some fish and chips, so she gave it to him. If she'd said no I don't suppose anything would have happened, but she said yes, and now she likes to think of herself as a victim of the latest crimewave . . .' He was laughing so much that he had to put down his tea.

'Well . . .' If he thought it was so funny, she was loathe to go on.

'Well what? Come on, you've had nothing but good ideas so far, let's hear it,' he insisted, watching her bemused face. She couldn't work out whether he was being genuinely friendly or patronising—and neither could he, Hal discovered with a jolt. He had hoped to treat Rosie Simpson with a degree of professional regard and nothing more. She really wasn't attractive enough to merit more than professional interest. There could be none of the physical excitement or the sense of a chase with such a girl. And yet he found himself quite genuinely enjoying her company, unsophisticated and untutored as she was. He stopped laughing and regained his composure.

'I thought that it might give some of the older people a bit more confidence if they had some knowledge of self-defence. Nothing strenuous, just so that they know the best moves to make if someone attacked them or something . . .'

The smile was beginning to tug at his lips again. 'Don't you think that's a bit strong?'

'Even in an area like this, as you say, with very little crime, a lot of them are frightened by what they see and hear on TV and in the papers. They really do worry about it, Dr Dickinson,' she murmured, uncomfortable with his name yet not daring to call him Hal.

Someone else he might have encouraged to use his Christian name, but Hal was biting back something within him, something too positive in his reaction to this lump of a young woman. His standards were high. He couldn't *really* be friends with a shy, clumsy, not very articulate nurse. He scolded himself. Because she was friendly and approachable and had none of Claire's bad habits he'd relaxed too much in her presence. Yet she had nothing to offer *him*. The practice—now that was different. She would be good for the practice, so he wouldn't antagonise her, but he wouldn't get close to her either. He carefully crossed his knees away from her. Rosie noted the gesture and leant back from him, sensing a change in his attitude, though she had no idea why. Was it something she had said? How was she to know that it was something in him that held him back, not in her?

'You've got a point,' he admitted distractedly. 'I suppose you had to learn basic self-defence up at Highstead, did you, just in case of trouble at night?'

'Just a few tricks, yes. I don't think anyone ever had to use them, mind you, but we all felt more confident because of it. So I thought that the same might be true of the older patients. If they thought that they would know what to do if someone broke into their house or approached them in the street . . .'

'I can just see Mrs Loach throwing some young bully over her shoulder,' Hal smiled. 'Yes, you're right Nurse Simpson. I suppose it's the police we ought to approach first for some advice, even if they can't do the teaching themselves. I don't suppose that even the Woodbridge police have had self-defence training. We'll have to bring in a crack squad from Ipswich at this rate.' And laughing still at the very idea of it, he stood up and left.

Rosie sat on in her sitting-room for another ten minutes before she had to go down for surgery. Whatever she had said or done this afternoon, it had created a deep rift between them, she could feel that. One moment he had been so friendly, so nice, his eyes laughing in appreciation of her and with genuine humour. And then suddenly those dark blue depths had been cold, unsharing, and she had felt herself cut out, a stranger in her own sitting-room. Except that it wasn't *her* sitting-room; it was his, just as everything around here seemed to be his. His ambition, his success, his organisation. Claire his girl-friend. The patients, even those who came to see her, *his* patients in some indefinable way. Without him she wouldn't be here . . . Oh yes, Hal Dickinson was a powerful, ambitious, driving man. And she was here as stalwart Rosie, not as a companion or a friend but as one of the cogs in Dr Dickinson's machine. He would humour her and be pleasant to her while she succeeded, while her ideas were good and her presence brought the place to life. But she could not expect anything more of such a man. The room suddenly felt cold. Her heart felt a deep chill. It had all looked so good, so promising, but all that had happened was that poor old Rosie had fallen once more for a handsome face and promising words. She had taken him not at face value but for what she imagined he *might* offer. And she knew with terrifying certainty that what she'd *really* hoped for from him could never, never be hers.

* * *

'It's my mother. She's not an elderly woman, but sometimes I think she's going senile.' The woman sitting in Rosie's chair dabbed a handkerchief to her cheek and resumed her story. 'I've been to Dr Higgins but he just thinks I'm exaggerating it all. He even asked me if I wanted tranquillisers. He thinks *I'm* going dotty but I'm not! So that's why I'm here, Nurse. No one else will sit and listen to me, I'm afraid. They'll none of them believe me when I tell them about Mother. But it's true.'

Rosie tried to look sympathetic, but her eyes couldn't help straying to the clock. It was gone eight. The last patient had left more than forty minutes ago.

'It's all right, Nurse Simpson, I'll be going.' Mrs Guthrie wiped her eyes and gathered her handbag. 'Dr Higgins was right, it'll probably seem better as soon as I've had a few tablets.'

Rosie didn't like defeatist talk like that. Nor did she like the idea of someone unwillingly taking tranquillisers when as far as they were concerned they had real cause for the distress they were feeling. 'No, don't go yet. I'd like to hear some more,' she said brightly.

Mrs Guthrie sat down with something like gratitude on her face. 'Honestly, just come and visit and you'll see for yourself what she's like. The community nurse came one day, but all she did was have a two-minute chat and then she almost accused me of being paranoid.'

Rosie held back an uncharitable thought and instead took out her pen and paper. 'How old is your mother, Mrs Guthrie?'

'She's sixty-two. Only nineteen years older than me.'

'And what would you say her symptoms are? I mean you've said you think she might be going senile, but *why* exactly?'

'She keeps dropping things. Well, that's nothing new, it's been going on for five or six years or more. But she doesn't seem to have any strength, Nurse Simpson. She'd often . . . well . . .' Mrs Guthrie leant over as if she was going to impart a great secret. 'She's incontinent at times, and her mind really does seem to wander. And then she has these spasms.'

'Spasms? Muscular spasms?' Rosie felt like a proper GP, sitting here taking notes. But if the others in the practice had washed their hands of Mrs Guthrie, why shouldn't she act the part?

'Convulsions almost. They leave her very confused. She talks to herself. She's been having these jerky movements for years, dropping things, but the doctor just says that everyone loses their co-ordination as they get a bit older . . .'

'Not to this extent they don't,' Rosie chipped in. She couldn't think what could possibly be wrong with Mrs Guthrie's mother, but it sounded rather more severe than the ordinary problems of increasing age. 'Has she had tests?' The only thing that sprang immediately to mind was multiple sclerosis —but there was no paralysis here, not as far as she could make out. And the muscle spasms sounded very odd.

'Yes, a few years ago. They thought at first she had Reynaud's disease—that's a circulation thing,' she added for Rosie's benefit, but Rosie already knew, and there was a silence as she digested the information. A vague seed of recognition of the symptoms nagged at the back of her mind, but she couldn't have said why for the life of her. Also a sense that maybe Mrs Guthrie might be imagining things began to invade her. If tests had been done and had proved clear . . .

'Obviously I can't give you any idea of what's happening and why. I'm not a doctor,' she said gently, 'and really it's up to them. But if you'd like to bring your mother in one day I'd happily have a chat with her. Or I could ask the community nurse to come round again and meet you both.' It didn't sound much of an offer, really, not when the poor woman was at her wits' end, but what else could she do?

'I'll bring Mother in to see you,' Mrs Guthrie said decisively, 'and then perhaps someone will take some notice of her. Can I have an appointment, Nurse? If I bring her in during ordinary hours and we have to wait for long she might make a nuisance of herself.'

Either Mrs Guthrie needed help herself, Rosie decided as she made a firm appointment, or her mother was suffering from a tragically early onset of senility . . . Or . . . It wouldn't come. The key that she felt would make sense of everything she'd heard this evening was there, but it wouldn't come. Rosie saw Mrs Guthrie out and then returned to clear up her room. She put away the spare crêpe bandage left after binding up a twisted ankle, and put the receiver she'd used to collect stitches from someone's healed hand in the steriliser. It had been an interesting evening on the whole. Two pregnancy tests, one brought in by a very worried-looking young girl who'd hardly looked her in the eye all the time they spoke, another by an equally worried woman in her thirties who was terrified that this would prove to be yet another false alarm.

Then there'd been a young man who'd walked the seven miles from Woodbridge in ill-fitting shoes in the early hours of the morning because he didn't have the taxi fare—and had ended up with a really shocking blister right across his instep. She'd had to break and clean and dress that, but the poor chap wouldn't be doing much walking for the next few days and he'd hobbled out on crutches. She'd taken blood samples for tests, at the bidding of Dr Higgins who thought that one of his patients might have hepatitis, and she'd done a quick internal examination of a panicked lady who wouldn't find the string of her new IUD and thought it had dropped out. It hadn't, as it turned out, and Rosie felt quite pleased that she'd been able to put the woman's mind at rest and teach her a little about her own body, all without bothering the doctors. She'd done a breast examination and shown the woman how to do it for herself, something which she knew, with pride, could save a life, and she'd given Veronica Reitz her anti-allergy injection. All in all it had been a good day's work, and far more varied and enjoyable than soothing fevered brows on a ward and waiting for Sister to come and take over.

Still, Mrs Guthrie intrigued and niggled, partly because Rosie hadn't been able to do anything for her. As she stood at the sink, carefully preparing the used syringes before she disposed of them in the special yellow plastic bag that was collected by the dustmen separately each week, her mind turned over the facts and the apparent symptoms. There *was* something familiar, something worrying about them. But what? Pulling off her rubber gloves and picking up the samples that were to be despatched to the lab in the morning. Rosie resolved to have a look in the Guthrie files and check out what had been noted all those years ago when the signs had first appeared.

Calling quickly in at Dr Higgins' room, where the fridge was kept, to drop her samples off, Rosie padded quietly into the reception area. The last patients had gone home half an hour ago—and so had everyone else, by the look of things. The front door was locked, but that was no problem as all the staff had keys. Security was absolutely necessary in these days when clinics were broken into for the few drugs kept on the premises. Rosie pulled out her keys and let herself into the rear part of the reception area, also kept locked when the place wasn't in use. This was where the files were kept; confidential files. There was sufficient light from the late evening sun for her to find the relevant folder and pull it from the special rotary rack system designed to make all patient files easily accessible—but she never quite got around to reading it.

From the corridor which led to the doctors' surgeries came the sound of Claire Kemp's laugh, and Hal's murmuring voice. Hidden from view by the thick glass of the reception desk and the dimness, Rosie watched them enter the reception area.

'I missed it.' Claire was laughing. 'I'm pleased to hear that it went well, but that's not why I'm so angry with myself.' She pulled a little face. Rosie withdrew into the shadows as Hal came up to the reception desk and laid a couple of letters on it for Mrs Hammond to post for him in the morning.

'Oh, then why *do* you feel deprived?' he asked

casually. He could almost predict what Claire was going to say, and he felt rotten for leading her on, but he didn't want her to think he was being soft on Rosie. He *wasn't* soft on Rosie, damn it! All the same, he didn't want to hear Claire running her down.

'Because I thought I'd give myself a giggle and have a look at our wonderful Nurse Simpson in her track suit,' Claire laughed. 'Oh don't look at me like that, Hal! I know that as far as you're concerned she's the best thing that's happened to this place since you arrived, but you must admit, she's hardly Miss Charm and Elegance 1986, is she?'

Hal couldn't bring himself to answer. He didn't want to play the two women off against each other and as far as he was concerned Claire wasn't exactly charming herself—though elegant, and attractive she most certainly was. She was also, he knew deep down, the type of woman that a man like him married. She was urbane and presentable and witty company. That really couldn't be said for poor Nurse Simpson. 'Hmm . . .' he replied non-committally.

'More like Miss Elephant 1986!' Claire roared at her own joke. Rosie cringed as if she'd been slapped full in the face and felt such shame and humiliation as she'd never known before in her life.

'Hah!' Hal couldn't bring himself to join in Claire's amusement but he wasn't going to make life difficult for himself by arguing. She'd taken such a strange dislike to the new nurse that whenever he spoke glowingly of Rosie's performance Claire was up in arms against him. He hated himself for being such a coward, but why should he defend Rosie? Why couldn't she defend herself? he asked himself desperately. And in many ways Claire was the one who deserved his sympathy. She was in the process of a messy divorce, dumped by her feckless husband, and she must in her heart know that, despite all her hopes, there was no chance of a long-term reconciliation. Not with him, or with Dick.

'Never mind, I shall get a chance to peek at her in her full glory next week. She's not going to melt away overnight, I don't suppose!' Claire giggled. 'Let's leave this horrid place and go for dinner. How about the Horse and Cart, Hal? And not one word more about the biggest and best nurse this side of the Wash.'

'All right. Let's go.' Hal cast an eye over the area, turned round to check he'd left his letters safely—and through the gloom of the office behind the glass, caught the gleam of Rosie's stunned eyes as she stood imperfectly hidden behind a filing cabinet. She saw the raw surprise in his face too, the sudden hooding of his heavy lids. And he saw her betrayed expression and the way in which she recoiled from his gaze. He paused; she saw him catch his breath. Then he took Claire firmly by the arm and led her away, one hand snaking around her back and clasping her tight to his side.

'Let's have a lovely evening together,' he heard himself saying automatically as he unlocked the surgery door.

Judas! His conscience nagged him all the way to the hotel, all the way through dinner, all the way home—it even nagged him as he lay alone in his bed, having refused Claire's offer of company for the night. He felt as if he had just sent a calf off to the slaughterhouse or an old dog off to the vet for the last time. Those brown eyes, full of pain and misery behind the glass kept appearing in front of him. How could he have done it? How could he possibly have been so cruel? And why, *why*, he asked himself in vain, did he give a damn anyway? Nurses were ten a penny, even nurses as good as Rosie . . . Still his conscience wasn't appeased, still it nagged and filled him with shame and remorse for those few unkind words. Not even unkind, he reminded himself. Claire was the one who had been unkind, not him. But he should have been better than Claire, he knew. He should have corrected her and stopped her.

It was three in the morning and he hadn't managed to get a single moment's sleep yet. Furious with himself, the world and even, most unreasonably, Rosie herself, he climbed out of bed and found the whisky bottle . . .

Rosie waited until they had gone and until Hal had carefully kept up the charade that he hadn't seen her by locking the door and checking to make sure that it was secure. Through the window she had seen him walk arm in arm with Claire down the narrow pavement, chatting away as if nothing had happened. As if he hadn't seen her. As if he hadn't been laughing at her . . .

She felt too deeply cut to cry about it. It was like a deep slash with a razor, so clean that at first the true damage didn't sink in. She automatically replaced the Guthrie file in the stack and let herself out of the office. Like a sleepwalker, her mind just replaying Claire's nasty words, she let herself out of the surgery, smiled good evening at a passing patient, and made her way to her own front door. Miss

Elephant 1986. And they thought it was funny to watch her in her track suit.

The tears caught up with her as she climbed the stairs, cursing every spare inch of her body, cursing life itself. Because if she wasn't fat they wouldn't have anything to laugh at her for. It was her own fault, she'd brought it on herself, she sobbed, self-recrimination mounting. How could she ever have expected people to like her and want to be friends when all they could see were her double chin and spare tyre. And for a time she'd begun to think that Hal Dickinson was nice. Even that he was fond of her in some way. Well, maybe he valued her for what she could bring to the health centre, but he certainly thought nothing of her as a person.

It was very lonely in the flat. Once she'd dried her eyes and changed out of her uniform into her smock dress she felt totally at a loss. She had no friends here, not even off-duty nursing friends to go along to the pub with. There was no television. An over-whelming sense of desertion made her shudder. Did anyone really care what happened to her? What were Hal and Claire saying about her in the Horse and Cart? The thought was too bitter to contemplate.

In the kitchen Rosie emptied the cupboards, taking down the box of pasta and the packet of chocolate biscuits. At the back of one cupboard she found a forgotten tin of rice pudding. Well, she could have that while the pasta cooked, and then she could follow it with the biscuits. She opened the fridge door. She would have butter and cheese and pepper on her pasta, and there was also half a can of baked beans to be finished off. She stood all the food on the worktop and surveyed it with something like pleasure. And then, before she had time to start thinking about Hal Dickinson or Claire Kemp again, she got to work with her can opener and spoon, and before long was feeling the comfort of food. People might forsake her and insult her, she thought as she finished the last of the creamed rice and tested the tagliatelle, but she would always find solace here. And Hal Dickinson she could do without!

CHAPTER SIX

THE moment that Mrs Astill, her last patient, left the surgery Rosie began to tidy up and get ready to hurry away. With any luck, Hal would still be closeted with a patient and she could leave the place without bumping into him. The memory of his hurtful words last night still rankled with her and she couldn't bear to come face to face with him—not for some time, anyway. He hadn't called her this morning or made any effort to apologise —but then, why should he? He couldn't know how dependent on his good opinion she felt, and it was obvious that he didn't care anything for her feelings.

The telephone rang just as she was about to leave and hurry back to her own flat, and she answered it hesitantly.

'Good, I've caught you.' Philip Higgins' voice was a relief. 'How did you get on with Mrs Astill? I'm sorry to offload her on to you, but she's been making my life very difficult in the last couple of weeks. Keeps coming in and begging me to tell her that she doesn't need to stay on the diet any more.'

'Oh, she was no trouble,' Rosie said cheerfully. 'I just went over the diet sheet again and tried to drum in why she mustn't have gluten. I think she understood, but she still keeps complaining about not being able to eat proper bread. She seems to think that if she complains and asks hard enough, we'll change the rule!'

'You're a good girl, Rosie. She's got another appointment with the consultant coming up soon, so maybe we can make a few changes after that. Right,' he laughed. 'I'm off for the weekend now. Hal's on call and I'm off to the bright lights. See you on Monday, my dear.'

Rosie had heard from Mrs Hammond that Dr Higgins had friends in London and got away there whenever he could. She wondered briefly what he did there, and why he'd chosen to work in such an out-of-the-way place if he really preferred the city. As far as she was concerned, the only drawback to working in the country was in the shape of Hal Dickinson.

The thought reminded her of her earlier intentions, and picking up her bag she trotted up the corridor and along to the reception desk, where she left her patient records for Claire or Mrs Hammond to put away. Claire was there and on the telephone, for which Rosie was heartily grateful. She didn't know whether she had it in her to be pleasant to the woman after the things she'd said last night.

There was just time to wash and change out of her uniform and have a bite of lunch before getting to the High Street for the afternoon bus into Woodbridge. Rosie felt her heart beat with excited pleasure at being free for the afternoon. She'd been into Woodbridge and into Ipswich before to get her furniture, but those visits had been for business and she'd caught only tantalising glimpses of woods and water and dozens of small yachts moored in the estuary from which rose the little market town. Today she'd explore properly and enjoy herself. There would be no patients with *their* problems, no Hal Dickinson and *no* Claire Kemp.

The bus pottered cautiously along the winding Suffolk roads, stopping to pick up stray passengers as it went. Rosie sat back and enjoyed the ride, for it was a lovely spring afternoon, with warm sunshine and a scudding breeze. The trees, newly in leaf, and the greenness of the fields and hedgerows left her feeling almost ridiculously happy. Woodbridge was a joy too, with its half-timbered cottages and wool exchange and the steep narrow streets. After buying a new supply of black tights and some basic groceries, she had tea in a pretty tea-shop and then wandered down to the river, mindful of the time of the bus for her return journey. There was only one bus going back to Clayburgh before eight this evening, she'd been told, so she'd better not miss it.

The estuary here was wide and blue and surrounded by wooded hills and shady inlets. The sailing fraternity were there in force, getting their boats ready and launching them back into the water after a winter on the land. There were so many of them bobbing about at anchor along the jetties that Rosie could barely believe her eyes. Carrying her purchases, she wandered down a footpath by the boat builders and the chandlery, out to the old mill, where she had a guided tour of its inner workings. She wasn't particularly interested in mills or their workings, but today there seemed to be a spell over everything; something magical hung in the air and everything she saw gave her delight.

Back at the bus stop though, things proved not to be at all magical. 'Clayburgh, you say?' The elderly man waiting there looked puzzled. 'I think that one's gone. They changed to the summer timetable the other week. You sure that it's not the old timetable you're working on?'

Another elderly Woodbridge resident on his way to Saxmundham confirmed that indeed, the bus that went directly through Clayburgh had gone. 'Next one's at six-thirty,' he said helpfully, consulting his timetable. 'Oh, no, that's in the other direction. Next one through Clayburgh is ten past eight. Not a very busy route, you see,' he said apologetically. 'You in a hurry?'

'Not really,' Rosie said half-heartedly, feeling the magical air of the afternoon beginning to disintegrate. The idea of a two-and-a-half-hour wait, even in this pleasant place, wasn't exactly what she'd planned.

'You could walk back from Burgholt crossroads if you catch the Southwold bus,' the first man suggested helpfully. 'They'd put her off there, wouldn't they? Then it's only a mile or so into Clayburgh.'

Both gentlemen agreed that this was a practical solution—indeed, the *only* solution if Rosie was going to get home much before nine, and so, armed with a home-made map drawn very faintly in pencil on the back of an old envelope, she clambered down from the Southwold bus at Burgholt crossing. There was nothing and no one around, but she'd been brought up in the country and the hedgerow noises and narrow lanes didn't bother Rosie. The sun was still shining warmly and she convinced herself that the exercise would do her good and burn off a few of the calories she'd consumed last night. Even so, the mile walk which the old gentlemen had insisted was just a doddle seemed much further to her feet. She wondered dryly if *they'd* ever walked the route themselves, or whether a mile in the country is by definition twice as far as a mile in the town.

The lane petered out at a narrow crossroads and Rosie consulted her map. Left here—or was it straight ahead? There was a signpost but it was propped against a hedge in a drunken fashion, pointing nowhere in particular. It had obviously been the victim of a hit and run accident, Rosie decided. She would go left, anyway, and see where that took her.

Around a bend she came across the first signs of habitation for some time. There were a couple of low pink-washed cottages, typical of the area. At first she'd been surprised at seeing so many pink cottages, but now they had become familiar in the Suffolk countryside. Further along she could see water, another of the myriad inlets in the area, secret creeks and rivers meandering their way across country. She passed a large house, part of a farm, with what looked like holiday homes with separate front doors created in the wings. And ten minutes on from there she came across another pretty cottage, white-washed this time, but with the same old black beams criss-crossing its frontage and a mass of terracotta pantiles on its roof. Across its garden came the familiar flash of dancing water, hidden for the time being by the clouds of apple blossom and new foliage in the burgeoning cottage garden.

How lovely to live here, right by the river, in this glorious old place. Rosie could imagine it inside, cosy and low-ceilinged, full of character and wonderfully peaceful in its gardens. So far only one car had passed her along the road. This place really was an idyllic backwater. Putting her shopping down for a moment on the low stone wall, she consulted her map again. She couldn't make out whether some of the lines on it were pencil marks or just folds in the paper, so faint was it. Maybe she should knock at this cottage, or go back to the farm up the road. After all, if she had taken a wrong turn it might take her miles out of her way.

At precisely that moment there was a distant metallic clang and then a figure appeared around the side of the house. It was a man, though more than that she couldn't tell because he was carrying what looked to her like a sail and one of the metal ropes attached to it was dragging noisily on the back garden path that snaked right round the house.

'Excuse me!' He didn't hear her. 'I'm sorry to disturb you . . .'

Hal thought he must be hearing things. He'd been up most of the night worrying about her and now he could hear Rosie's voice hailing him. He shook his head and continued to lug the canvas up the garden. 'Excuse me! Could you tell me the way to Clayburgh?' It was quite unmistakable this time. He dropped the damp canvas, which had been covering his boat for the winter, and turned to take a look at the road. And there she was, quite without doubt. Discomfort at meeting her again so soon after last night's fiasco threatened to overcome him, but instead he strode down the garden path to the front wall. The look of horror that passed over her face as she recognised him confirmed that he was the very last person she wanted to bump into.

Rosie instinctively picked up her straw shopping bag and clutched it to her bosom. 'Oh, it's you,' was all she could say blankly.

'Hello, come to visit or did I hear you say that you were lost?' Hal smiled brightly, just failing to meet her eyes. Her embarrassment humbled him. What should he say? Maybe he should apologise, but then that might make her feel even worse. She probably preferred to forget that it had ever happened.

'I didn't know you lived here, otherwise I . . .'

'Otherwise you wouldn't have come within a mile of the place,' Hal finished gently. 'I'm sorry, Rosie.'

Rosie regarded her dusty feet. As apologies went it was hardly profuse, and yet there was a depth to his voice and a sudden sincerity that made her spine tingle. She believed him, though she knew that she'd believe anything he told her, regardless of whether it was true or not.

'I missed the bus from Woodbridge, so they put me of at Burgholt. I was supposed to be able to walk from there but I seem to have taken a wrong turning.' She looked up at him for the first time and saw him patient and listening in front of her. There was something in his dark blue eyes she couldn't fathom, until she realised how grubby and untidy she must look. She'd collected some of the most common wildflowers as she'd passed the hedges and now she had dandelions and a few bits of blossom protruding from her shopping bag and looking rather wilted. He was probably feeling sorry for her—if he wasn't having a silent chuckle at her expense.

'They must be mad,' he said calmly after a moment. 'It's more than three miles to Burgholt. You're in the right direction for Clayburgh but you've still got more than a mile to go.'

'That way?' Rosie nodded in the direction she'd been going in anyway.

'Yes, but . . .' Hal wasn't sure whether to stop her or not. He'd hurt her, he could see that from her shy brown eyes and the unusually stubborn tightness of her mouth, usually so generous. Should he stop her or let her show her independence by walking on?

'Come back—at least come in and sit down for a few minutes. I'll make a cup of tea. Then you can go on if you insist, or I'll run you back.' He blurted it all out quickly, but she determinedly set off along the road again. She kept walking and he bounded along on the inside of the wall, keeping pace with her but divided by the wall and the herbaceous border. 'Rosie, please, don't be silly. You must be exhausted. Please, come in and have a cup of tea with me. It won't take a minute.' For heaven's sake, he thought, why was he doing this? Why was he standing here *begging* this woman to stop?

'It's all right, thanks. I'm okay,' she insisted, aware of him walking with her. 'I don't want to be a nuisance.'

Because a nuisance is exactly what I am, she thought with a touch of self-pity as she strode on. A cup of tea would be lovely. And the idea of having a look at Hal Dickinson's house was almost irresistible—almost, but not quite. What had he called her yesterday? The biggest nurse this side of the Wash? Well, maybe *he* hadn't called her that, but he'd agreed with Claire when she had. Pride wouldn't let her stop. She simply didn't have the confidence to face the man who might value her for her nursing but found the idea of her in a track suit suitable cause for humour.

'Now look . . .' Hal vaulted over the garden wall and stopped her in her tracks by grabbing her shoulders. She was aware of the salt smell of him and the way his hair was tangled by the stiff breeze. He must have been out sailing, she thought in the split second before he turned her, surprised and unaware of what to do, around. 'This is ridiculous. You've walked miles carrying your shopping and you won't even come into my kitchen for a cup of tea. As your employer I insist you at least sit down for five minutes before going on.'

It was a feeble excuse, and he knew it, but he was not going to let her just walk off like that. He entertained her with the history of the house as he guided her up the garden path. Rosie remembered another time when he had led her along like this, back home in Devon, and a sigh escaped her involuntarily. It had all been before her then; she had arrived with such high hopes of a friendship with him, but now . . .

'Have you been sailing?' she asked stupidly, too flummoxed to think of anything more sensible.

'Yes, just for an hour or two down the estuary. My first time out this year. It's glorious,' he responded. 'Do you sail, Rosie? Maybe you'd like to come out?'

'Me?' Her astonished gaze delighted him, for it was the first real response he'd got out of her in the last five minutes of banal chit-chat. 'I don't think that's a very good idea.'

Hal couldn't help but smile on her with one of those momentary grins that had throughout his entire life brought instant forgiveness from whoever he had offended. 'Rosie,' he exclaimed with exasperation, pulling off his Wellingtons at the back door, 'you are your own worst enemy. Why don't you think it's a good idea? Can you swim? Do you get seasick or something?'

'I can swim,' she admitted gravely, 'and I don't get seasick. But I'm not really the right sort of person to go sailing.'

'You don't have to be "the right sort of person" to do anything! Come in to my parlour.' He opened the back door with ceremony and ushered her in, continuing his lecture. 'You mustn't get too stuck in the image that other people put you in. Nurses are expected to be all sweetness and light, and it drives some of them mad to be that way. You should be who you are and do what you want.' He was tactful enough, Rosie thought with gratitude, not to suggest that her reason for not wanting to get into his boat was fear that she might sink it. 'When you were in Woodbridge this afternoon did you go down to the jetties and yards?'

'Yes, it's beautiful down there,' she agreed. 'I walked around for some time.' She could barely take her eyes off his economical movements as he filled the kettle and set it on the Aga.

'And didn't you think it might be nice to go sailing?' He fixed her with a lazy, cynical eye that already knew the answer.

'Well, yes. But it was only an idea. Don't you ever wonder about doing things you wouldn't really do in real life?' Her defiance merely raised another lazy grin.

'Stop trying to avoid the question, Nurse Simpson. All I'm saying to you is that you need to have a bit more confidence in yourself. You've got yourself marked down as a 'Can't do' person, which is ridiculous because so far everything you've set your hand to you've done exceptionally well. You went green when I asked you to start that pensioners' class and yet you took it on and it was a big success.'

'It kept everyone amused at least,' Rosie muttered bitterly, unable to hold the words back. She felt her eyes stinging and was terrified for a moment that she was going to cry, so she picked up a teaspoon that had been left on the table and began to run her fingers over its cool surface.

'Oh, Rosie . . .' His voice was very nearly a whisper. 'I've been feeling so bad about that. I'm sorry. Look at me.' He'd never in his life before wanted to gather someone up and kiss them gently, kiss away the hurt rather as one might do with a small child, but he did now. Because he instinctively knew how much he'd betrayed her. It was stupid to get all paternal like this—to feel protective towards a great lump of a girl who should by now have learned to shrug off petty insults, but he couldn't help it. Something in her brought out the caring side of him. Some sort of brotherly sympathy, though heaven knew why.

Rosie steadfastly stared at the teaspoon. She couldn't look him in the eye because she wasn't sure what would happen if she did. Maybe she'd cry. Maybe she'd make an even worse fool of herself.

'You're a total idiot,' Hal said gently, bending down to stroke her hectic brown curls. And then, without thought, he smoothed back her hair, lifted it and placed a simple kiss at the nape of her neck. She was warm and smooth and smelt of baby talc and shampoo, so he kissed her gently again. 'And now,' he murmured shakily, overcome by the gesture, 'I'll make that tea.'

Rosie stared out of the kitchen window and wondered whether she might not have died without knowing it. Or had she imagined that he had kissed her? So maybe it wasn't the greatest, most passionate kiss of all times, but could he actually have kissed her? And now what was she going to say to him? A horrible thought occurred to her, a memento of her last kiss, the last time she'd decided that she was in love. That had been with Giles Levete, and he'd given her a kind goodnight kiss on her doorstep when she'd supplied him with information about Sister Slater. *That* kiss had led to all sorts of trouble and frustration. Was this going to lead to the same thing?

'Here you are.' Hal sat down beside her and handed her a blue and white striped mug of tea. 'Okay?' It was the kind of question that didn't need a reply, so she just nodded and tried not to let on how her heart was pounding, half with fear and half with pleasure.

They sat in silence for a while, watching the sun going down over the hill on the other side of the small inlet. Hal's garden was long, at least two hundred yards, and sloped very gradually to the water through an old orchard of fruit trees. Nearer the house there was a formal lawn and a walled area, with the wisteria and roses just beginning to come to life after their long sleep. The place was beautiful; slightly wild, certainly no tulips standing in neat rows. And his kitchen, Rosie decided, feeling bold enough to look round, was pretty much the same. An old scrubbed pine table at which they were sitting, an elderly Aga, a few fitted units but mainly pine shelves. Squeezed in one corner was a battered Welsh dresser. It was comfy, attractive and unpretentious. Somehow it didn't seem to fit with the Hal she'd met at work. He seemed so concerned that everything be done neatly and properly; he was so efficient. And yet wasn't he concerned that the health centre should reflect welcome warmth? That it should be a home from home so that people could come in and relax, rather than dreading a long wait in a draughty waiting room? It *did* begin to make sense.

'Have you always lived in Suffolk?' she asked suddenly.

'Good grief no! I worked in London for a long time, in a fairly run-down area in the inner city, Tower Hamlets. But no matter how hard I worked there, I didn't seem to be able to make a dent in the problems.' He frowned and sat back in his chair, tilting it on two legs. 'You don't want to hear about that.'

'I would like to.' Rosie waited expectantly.

'There's not a great deal to tell. You've worked in a big London hospital, you know what it's like. There are days when you seem to have had most of London through your doors, and half their problems aren't things you can help with. A doctor can't prescribe medicine to help people who live in over-crowded conditions or do anything to help a family scraping along on a pittance.'

'Some people bring it on their own heads,' Rosie interrupted. 'The Casualty department's always full of people who've drunk too much and had accidents, that sort of thing. It's very frustrating trying to help people get better if you know they're just going to go out and do the same thing again.'

'Exactly.' Hal tipped forward again and finished

the last of his tea. 'So a couple of years ago I began looking around for a GP practice to build up, somewhere where we could do our best to offer as much back-up and support to the community as possible. That reminds me,' he rose and fetched a pencil and paper, 'I think we ought to have an arthritis clinic. And I also want to do some relaxation classes. A friend of mine from London has used them with some of his patients and staff with great effect. He's taught me the techniques, so I'll have a go here. I want you to keep a note of anyone whose problem seems to stem more from general tension and stress than physical problems.'

'It's total health care, really,' Rosie nodded, her head on one side. 'It sounds perfect, but you're going to have to rely on tremendous dedication from your team, aren't you?'

Hal smiled wryly and gave a short sigh. 'That's the one thing I can't rely on, I know. I've made a couple of mistakes already with the . . .'

There was a loud thumping at the front door. He shrugged and, still in damp jeans and socks, padded out to the hall. Rosie heard an anxious male voice, Hal's calm, 'Yes, I'll come now,' and she began to gather up her things.

'How are your obstetrics?' he asked as he came back into the kitchen and went to collect his boots.

'Babies? I haven't really delivered one since . . . well, years ago. Somehow I didn't find that it interested me. It's all so technical and you can't get to know your patients,' Rosie admitted shamefacedly.

'The perils of modern medicine,' Hal laughed. 'Well, come with me, help deliver this baby and

then I'll run you home.' He fished around in the
pocket of his green jacket, which was made of oiled
canvas, and came up with his bleeper. 'I'll take this,
just in case anyone else needs me. Are you ready,
Rosie?'

'Aren't you going to change? What's she going
to think when you turn up at the bedside in
your jeans? Not that you . . .' Rosie blushed yet
again and was silent. How could she tell him how
handsome he looked, how dark and dashing and
masculine?

'This particular mother won't mind. Come on!'
With a twinkle in his eye, Hal lead her around to
the car. 'There are Wellingtons for you in the back
seat,' he remembered as they emerged from the
drive. 'They'll be too big, but you can stuff some
tissues in the feet.' He handed her a box of tissues
from the glove compartment. 'I always carry the
biggest pair around, then no one ever gets caught
out.' Rosie said nothing, merely stuffed half a box
of the tissues into each boot and wondered why
they were needed. Eventually she plucked up
courage to ask.

'We're going to a farm, and it's pretty mucky.
Best to have boots on,' Hal laughed, and again
there was that infuriating twinkle in his eye. It was
still there a few minutes later when they drove up
and parked in the farmyard. Rosie had expected
the place to be half-buried in muck, but it looked
reasonably clean. So much for the wellies! But
before she could make tracks for the farmhouse,
Hal called her over towards some low-built sheds at
one side of the yard.

'In there? Is this some kind of joke?' Rosie
hung back, but Hal's firm hand on her shoulder

persuaded her to enter. 'Here's our patient,' he grinned, walking over to a beautiful Jersey cow lying straining in the straw of the cow-shed.

'No joke, I promise.' Hal turned to the farmer standing at the cow's side and exchanged a few words. Rosie watched in silence as he examined the animal, then stood up again. 'It's taking its time, but there's nothing wrong as far as I can see,' he said calmly. 'We'll give her a while longer.' He washed his hands thoroughly in the buckets of hot water that stood in a line waiting, and came back to Rosie with a crooked grin.

'Maybe I should inform the BMA that you're moonlighting as a vet,' she laughed, watching him drying his forearms, with a gritty old towel faded to a dull yellow colour by continual washing. Everything about him attracted her. It was madness to find oneself avidly watching a man's hairy wrists or the outlines of his strong knees as he bent down in his jeans, but she couldn't prevent herself. She could though, Rosie decided, prevent herself from ever showing him that she was interested, that she cared. No matter what he did or said, she wasn't going to make a fool of herself. She would never give him cause to amuse Claire with tales of how Nurse Simpson made eyes at him.

'Don't you dare.' That smile danced around his lips. He was like a boy whose joke had been well-received; but there was more to it than that, for Hal himself didn't know quite what made him feel so elated. There was something about Rosie, so appreciative, so willing, that gave what she did an extra dimension. Claire wouldn't have wanted to come in the first place. She certainly wouldn't have put on those Wellingtons without a barrage of

questions about who'd worn them last and the state
of their feet, and she would probably never have
entered the cow-shed door. Love him as she said
she did, her presence in his life simply made things
difficult. Whereas with Rosie there were no
questions, just quiet trust.

Hal watched her now, totally out of place in her
flowered frock and huge boots, crouched by the
cow's side, stroking her heaving belly. If only she
was beautiful. She had a gentle charm about her,
but no one in their right mind could really call Rosie
Simpson desirable.

Rosie looked up and caught the blank, bleak
look on his face. 'What's wrong?' Her question
threw him for a moment, then he pushed his dark
thoughts aside. 'Nothing. I was just wondering how
long the vet's going to be. I'd prefer him to handle
this if he's available. Caroline here is the family pet
and I wouldn't want anything to go wrong.' Hal's
hand stroked the animal's flank too, smoothing the
creamy coat. 'I've only been called in because the
local vet's off somewhere and his locum can't be
contacted.'

'Have you had a lot of experience with cows?'
Rosie wasn't quite sure whether it was all a big joke
or whether he often did this.

'I used to work on a farm in the school holidays
and the general points to look out for are the same
in cows as they are in human beings, so I'm better
than nothing. But I can't really tell if she's been in
labour too long. Kit,' he nodded to the man who'd
returned to the house to see if there was any sign
of the vet, 'just came down to ask my advice.
They don't keep many cows here, as I said. This
one's just a pet to give milk for the family, so he

doesn't have enough experience to know what's happening.'

'She's straining very hard, and the calf is moving. The contractions are getting quite strong,' Rosie laid her hand on Caroline's side and felt the muscular spasm. 'Is she dilated?'

'Nowhere near enough. How's her heart?' Taking his stethoscope from the bag he'd brought with him and carefully placed on a clean bale, Hal listened to the heartbeats of both mother and calf. 'There's no foetal distress as far as I can tell,' he concluded. 'There's really nothing I can do. The drugs I've got won't speed anything up. Let's get her on her feet for a minute.'

With Rosie pulling at the halter and Hal urging her from behind, Caroline got to her feet. She mooed plaintively once or twice, then seemed to breathe more easily. Rosie stayed by her side, talking and patting her. She'd never had a great deal to do with farm animals before, but having grown up in the countryside she wasn't scared of them. Besides, Jerseys were the most shy and delightful creatures around.

'Progress!' Hal's triumphant call shook her out of her thoughts. 'She won't be long now. Let her lie down again if she wants to.'

Fifteen minutes later, with the family's children watching and very blasé about the facts of life, the calf was born. Hal provided a little assistance with its legs, but apart from that he stood back with Rosie and watched. 'Poor Caroline,' Rosie sympathised afterwards, as she stroked the cow's neck in a farewell gesture. 'Fancy having to do that in front of an audience!'

'Thank you very much, Caroline,' Hal breathed

in her elegant silky ear. 'It comes naturally to you, even if it doesn't to me.'

He patted her too, and for a brief moment his hand found Rosie's among the tufted hair at the cow's neck. 'And well done, Rosie, too,' he added quietly. 'Who could ever ask for a more helpful midwife?'

The journey back into Clayburgh was silent. Rosie was deep in thought. First, she couldn't be sure whether the little gestures he'd made today were romantic or just attempts to boost her confidence and renew her loyalty to the health centre after last night's upsetting scene. She felt sure that Hal was genuine, but he was obviously the brains and heart behind the whole health centre project. If he thought a kiss and a few kind words would smooth things over, it was in his interest and quite within his thespian powers to carry out the plan. No matter how much she wanted it to be true, she couldn't believe that he really felt anything for her; not for herself, anyway. For her as a nurse, as a midwife to cows, maybe. But she was only to aware of her shortcomings in all those other areas that men found so important—in looks and flirtation and sophistication.

Hal's mind was playing with the same ideas and failing to come up with a reasonable answer too. He dropped her off at the health centre with a cheerful wave and more thanks for her help. 'See you on Monday!' he called as he reversed the car in the little parking space and disappeared down the road. He needed time on his own, time to work things out. He needed time to talk himself back into sanity, for the things he found himself contemplating were totally ridiculous. He would call Claire

and ask her over for dinner. Maybe her company
would sort him out; maybe a night spent with Claire
would convince him that she really *was* the woman
he wanted.

CHAPTER SEVEN

'I DON'T like the look of this.' Rosie pressed the slightly swollen flesh around the cut on Mr Wilson's arm and felt him wince. 'You've kept it nice and clean, but even so I think it's septic. When did you do it?'

'A couple of days ago. It wasn't deep and I washed it thoroughly, but it's been getting very hot and throbbing, so the wife told me to come and see you.' He looked at her nervously. 'What'll you have to do?'

'I'm going to get your doctor to come and see it, just for a second opinion, and if he agrees with me we'll give you a shot of antibiotic. Nothing to worry about,' Rosie said reassuringly, picking up the phone. Mr Wilson had gone pale but said nothing. 'It's Dr Higgins you normally come to see, isn't it?' she checked. Mr Wilson just nodded dumbly. He obviously thought that he was going to lose his arm, Rosie thought with some amusement as she dialled Philip Higgins' extension and explained the situation to him. He agreed to come across as soon as he had dealt with his present patient.

'There's really nothing to worry about,' Rosie tried to reassure her own patient. 'The antibiotics will fight the infection and the cut will heal up normally.'

'Is there any blood involved?' the man asked nervously.

'No, none at all. Maybe just a tiny pinprick. Are

124

you frightened of injections, Mr Wilson?' Rosie did her best to sound sympathetic. In hospital she'd met many a great bruising he-man who'd paled at the sight of the needle.

'No. It's just that my wife, well, Nurse, she's a Jehovah's Witness. I'm not,' he added quickly, 'but I'd have to think twice about anything that involved blood and transfusions because she wouldn't like it. Sorry,' he added lamely.

'Fortunately there's no need to worry,' Rosie said reassuringly. It was always a great dilemma to know what to do in such cases. People who held strong beliefs often avoided going to a doctor, even when they knew they were very ill, for fear of what the treatment might involve. In such cases the medical staff simply had to co-operate with the patient's wishes, however frustrated and angry they felt at the knowledge that they *could* help someone if only they were allowed to.

Dr Higgins, large and friendly, arrived, took a quick look at the cut and authorised an antibiotic jab to be followed by a short course of tablets. 'It's a good job we caught it before it got any worse,' he commented as he left. 'Come and see either Nurse Simpson or me if the symptoms persist, Mr Wilson. And please come back for us to take a look at it in five days' time, even if it begins to heal up.'

'Right, Doctor,' he agreed and rolled up his sleeve for Rosie to give him the jab. He took it stoically, allowed Rosie to dress it with special non-stick gauze and went on his way. The lady who came in as he left was less calm. She bundled a small child into the room in front of her and sat down as if she was to impart some terrible news.

'I couldn't bring myself to see Dr Dickinson.

What would he think?' she whispered across the desk when Rosie had finished clearing up from the last job.

Rosie adopted her tactful manner. Obviously this was something difficult. She racked her brains for the pregnancy tests she'd sent off to the lab recently. Had this lady's been amongst them? Had she found herself pregnant in inconvenient circumstances?

'It's nits,' the woman said so quietly that Rosie missed it. Her questioning look brought further disclosures, but not before the woman had turned to check that the door was shut and had leaned across the desk so that her mouth was only a few inches from the nurse.

'*Nits*. Some of the children had them at school, and I was combing through Kirsty's hair this morning and I found some.' Her face expressed her horror. 'What am I going to do? I don't want anyone thinking we're dirty, because I wash the children's hair twice a week . . .'

'That might have something to do with the problem, because nits prefer nice clean hair to dirty hair,' Rosie smiled gently. Little Kirsty's anxious face lightened. She'd obviously thought the end of the world had come when her mother had started making so much fuss. 'Come and sit on my lap for a minute, Kirsty,' Rosie invited, and nervously the child did so, allowing Rosie to comb through her blonde curls. Sure enough, she was quite heavily infested.

'I'd like to take some details so that our community nurse can go back to the school and try to clear this problem up,' Rosie insisted, although Kirsty's mum would really have preferred total anonymity. Gradually Rosie winkled out facts; the school, the class, when they'd last had their hair gone through. 'I'll make sure that you're visited at school in the next few days,' she promised, filing the information in the appropriate tray. 'Now, what are we going to do about you, Kirsty? Have you got brothers and sisters?'

The child nodded gravely. 'I've got two sons, ten and eight,' the woman explained. 'Do you reckon they've got them too?'

'It's possible. I can get the doctor to write you a prescription for a shampoo or I can give you the details and you can just go and buy it yourself. Which would you prefer, Mrs Nixon?' Having made so much fuss about the problem, Rosie could guess.

'I'll go and buy it myself, thank you. I don't want Doctor to know about this, Nurse Simpson, if you don't mind. Can I get it in Woodbridge?'

'You can probably get it here in Clayburgh,' Rosie said absently as she wrote the brand name of the lotion down on her pad.

'Oh no! And have everyone in the shop know about it!' Mrs Nixon was shocked at the very idea. 'In fact I'll probably go into Ipswich, to the big chemist there, just to be on the safe side.'

Rosie held back her smile at such old-fashioned prurience—but then she hadn't lived in a village for long enough to understand how quickly gossip and rumour could spread. Maybe the stigma had gone out of nits in London, where ethnic and housing problems had made nits an almost permanent feature of the landscape, but out here it was still considered a terrible disgrace.

'When you've got it, read the instructions on the

box and carry them out properly, otherwise it won't work,' Rosie instructed. 'And wash the whole family's hair with it, not just the children's, because you could all be infested. It's very easy for the entire family to suffer.' Mrs Nixon nodded as if in shock.

'I'm going to go and clean the entire house. The place won't know what's hit it,' she said firmly.

'Do it by all means, if it makes you feel better, but you won't be able to clean away the problem like that. And don't get too upset about it, Mrs Nixon. This sort of thing happens all the time and, as I said, it's the cleanest people who seem to worry about it most. There's really no need to go around disinfecting and shining everything in sight, I promise.' But Rosie could see that her message hadn't sunk in as, clutching the important piece of paper and shielding little Kirsty from the prying eyes outside, Mrs Nixon bustled out.

'Come in, Mrs Guthrie.' Rosie quickly got up to fetch another chair for the elderly lady who came in clinging to her daughter's arm.

'This is my mother, Mrs Norris,' Mrs Guthrie explained when they had her settled and Rosie had poured the tea she'd prepared. She had planned everything purposely. A cup of tea would test Mrs Norris's co-ordination and help them relax and chat. In this way she hoped to be able to judge how vaild Mrs Guthrie's claims were.

They started chatting about life in the village and how Mrs Norris must have seen it change, though Rosie had to keep constantly reminding herself that although this woman seemed as decrepit as a poorly eighty-year-old she was only just past retirement age. She'd certainly aged very badly. It soon became clear that Mrs Guthrie had not exaggerated the problem of her loss of memory—Mrs Norris could barely recall things she'd just said. Her mind wandered all the time and she sat staring around with surprise at her surroundings for the entire half-hour she was in the surgery. Occasionally she called out—usually about something that Rosie couldn't understand—or raised her arms against some invisible presence. Mrs Guthrie sat quietly by her side and tried to prompt rational chat, but very little was forthcoming.

'Have a cup of tea, Mrs Norris.' Rosie proffered the cup and the old lady made a clumsy swipe for it before Mrs Guthrie had time to catch her arm.

'She'll break the saucer—she won't be able to manage it. And she has such difficulty swallowing . . .' she began to explain.

'I'd like to see for myself,' Rosie said calmly, and placed the half-empty cup into the older woman's hand. She raised it to her mouth jerkily, much as a small child might. Then Rosie grabbed tissues and held them under Mrs Norris's chin as tea began to gurgle and dribble from the sides of the cup.

When they'd mopped her up, Rosie did a quick examination. The thing she was most interested in was Mrs Norris' reflexes, which seemed very slow or were non-existent. Had Philip Higgins done the same and not found cause for concern in the result? Surely she ought to have been referred to a specialist, even if the case did look like a classic one of senile dementia?

'I'm going to have a word with the doctor and with the community nurse,' she promised Mrs Guthrie as she and her mother pottered out. 'At the very least she ought to be seen by a specialist who'll be able to confirm that there's nothing out of the ordinary wrong with her.' Mrs Norris had begun to shake as Rosie spoke, and soon her limbs were moving in jerky spasms that almost brought her and her daughter to the floor.

'It's one of her convulsions,' Mrs Guthrie explained breathlessly as they brought the old lady back into the surgery and placed her on the couch. Rosie picked up the telephone and called Philip Higgins immediately. Whatever this was, it wasn't just a case of someone's arteries hardening before their time. It was something serious.

'What have you got for me now, Rosie, my dear?' Dr Higgins strode through the door with a broad smile on his face—a smile that disappeared at the sight of Mrs Guthrie and the prone Mrs Norris, who was still twitching. Rosie had fixed the oxygen mask over her face to assist her breathing, which had become very laboured, but the old lady's hands scrabbled at it frantically, trying to tear it off. 'Mrs Guthrie *and* Mrs Norris. What brings you here?' He sounded faintly defensive.

'Mrs Guthrie brought Mrs Norris in to have a cup of tea and a chat, but she's unfortunately had a convulsion. I really feel that she ought to be taken into hospital just for a check-up. She hit herself quite badly when she fell,' Rosie lied. What had induced her to say that? she wondered as Philip made a peremptory examination of the woman. She hadn't hit herself; but maybe Dr Higgins would feel more inclined to dispatch her to hospital if he thought she might have come to harm on his premises.

'I don't think there's any need for that, is there,

Mrs Norris?' he said coolly as he put down her wrist when he'd finished taking her pulse. 'Her breathing and pulse are back to normal and her heart's surprisingly strong for a woman of her age.'

'She's only sixty-two, Doctor,' Rosie reminded him and hoped she hadn't overstepped the mark.

'Any history of alcohol problems or schizophrenia in your family?' he asked Mrs Guthrie point-blank. Rosie blanched. She hadn't thought of that sort of thing. She'd assumed it was one of the diseases of old age that was causing the problem. But come to think of it, the symptoms *could* be explained by that.

'No!' Mrs Guthrie was shocked. 'No, Doctor, nothing like that at all. She lives with me, so I'd know if she was drinking. And she's never had any mental problems—not until all this started and her mind began to wander.'

'It's all right, don't get steamed up,' Philip muttered, rather callously, in Rosie's opinion. 'I've got to check out all the possibilities, that's all. Well, I can't see much wrong with her now. She's just getting old, Mrs Guthrie. You've simply got to accept that fact and learn to live with it. There's nothing we doctors can do to reverse the ageing process, I'm afraid. If we knew how to we'd all be millionaires.'

'But Dr Higgins, she's just had a convulsion. I saw it myself. I really do think we ought to get her scanned at the hospital. This kind of behaviour isn't typical of a woman of her age and we should investigate it.' Rosie's voice was as firm as it could be. She didn't have the natural authority of Sister Slater maybe, but when she felt strongly about something she simply had to make her voice heard.

'And what do you think it might be?' Philip
Higgins' eyes glowered at her for interfering. 'You
have a great deal of geriatric experience, I
suppose? Let's have your diagnosis, Nurse
Simpson.'

Rosie stood at the centre of the room, attentive
eyes all round her. Dimly at the back of her mind
she could feel Mrs Norris' symptoms striking a
chord with something she'd once read. The name of
the disease was like a tickling itch that she couldn't
quite scratch. What could it possibly be?

'I think it might be Huntington's chorea. All the
symptoms are there.' Like a flash it came to her,
and before she could debate the wisdom of the
diagnosis it was out on the air—and Philip Higgins
was laughing at her, his hands on his hips and his
mouth wide open in surprise.

'You really think that Mrs Norris might be
suffering from a very rare genetic problem, do you?'
he said through his laughter.

'The symptoms are all there—gradual loss of
co-ordination throughout the fifties, jerky movements . . .' The article she had read in a nursing
magazine began to come back to her now with
startling clarity. 'Behaviour that might be interpreted as drunken or bizarre, and then the gradual
breakdown to dementia or even insanity, along
with loss of physical control. Yes, I think it might be
Huntington's,' she said firmly. 'I've never seen
anyone of Mrs Norris' age like this before.'

Philip Higgins stared at her glassily for a few
moments, then turned with a forced smile to Mrs
Guthrie. 'I'm afraid that Nurse Simpson has got her
facts confused, Mrs Guthrie,' he said apologetically. 'We certainly shouldn't be standing here

talking about your mother while she lies here uncomfortably. I'll prescribe some pills for you to give to her to make her a little easier to handle. See if they help. If they don't, come back to me and I'll try something else. Simply because we can't come up with a snap diagnosis to explain your mother's ills doesn't mean that we can't help you.'

He filled out the prescription and with the terse announcement that he had other patients waiting, left them.

'Do you really think she should go into hospital?' Mrs Guthrie asked plaintively. 'What was that you said she might have? Were you serious?'

'Yes. Well, I think she should at least be seen by a specialist. Huntington's chorea is very rare as Dr Higgins said, but it might explain some of your mother's problems. It's very unethical talking to you like this, I'm afraid, Mrs Guthrie. Neither I nor Dr Higgins should have discussed the problem so freely . . .'

'I'm very glad you did, Nurse,' the older woman said fiercely. 'I've spent three years trying to get someone to take the problem seriously—first with the old doctor who was here and then with Dr Higgins—and not once has someone actually suggested that there might be a real cause. That's the problem with doctors. They never tell you what they think. They seem to expect you to be a mind-reader.'

Rosie gazed at the elderly lady lying on the plastic-covered examination couch. She was quiet now, exhausted by her convulsion, but soon she'd be exhibiting her bizarre behaviour all over again. And no one, it seemed, was prepared to take it seriously or do anything about it.

'I'm going to ring the hospital and try to persuade them to take her in,' she decided impulsively. 'I'll say that she's had a convulsion and that she needs investigating. And if necessary I'll say I'm calling on Dr Higgins' behalf.'

'Would you really?' Mrs Guthrie's eyes lit up with hope.

Rosie picked up the telephone.

Hal paced the floor of the flat with his hands rammed hard into the pockets of his trousers. 'You just picked up the phone and arranged for her to be taken in?' Rosie, seated on the sofa and hardly daring to move, let alone speak, nodded. 'It's quite amazing—not just your behaviour, which I can't begin to condone, but the fact that they actually found a bed for her. But you shouldn't have done it.'

'What do you think I *should* have done then? Just sent them both home, even when it was obvious that there was something seriously wrong with Mrs Norris that needs explaining?' Rosie's defiance caught Hal on the raw. After all, Philip had behaved with less dedication and concern than the case seemed to merit. Even so, that hardly justified Rosie's decision to take it into her own hands.

'You don't know that there's anything wrong with her at all,' he countered.

'But they're going to keep her in and the consultant is going to do tests, which shows that they don't think the case is a waste of time,' Rosie reminded him hotly. 'You keep going on about having the best interests of the patient at heart, and yet when I do something for a patient you accuse me of going over Dr Higgins' head.'

'You can't possibly deny that that's what you've done. He wanted her sent home . . .'

'He just wasn't going to do anything about her, and sending her home was the easiest way of washing his hands of the whole thing. I don't understand,' Rosie cried. 'You're so concerned about the elderly and their problems, yet you're not angry with him for what he's done!'

Hal's dark eyes flashed as he turned on her. 'I didn't say that. Philip already knows that I think he acted unwisely in the case. But that didn't give you an excuse to act over his head.' He sighed and ran his hand through his hair. His gut reaction was to side with Rosie and just be thankful that someone had done something about what was obviously a difficult situation. But as a doctor he couldn't allow his nurse to run the surgery.

'I really can't understand all the fuss,' Rosie said quietly, ashamed of her earlier outburst. 'Mrs Guthrie brought her problem to me and I felt that I could solve it for her.'

'You could have told me. I would have backed you up, from what I already know of the case,' Hal responded with equally quiet conviction. 'It doesn't matter if Philip and I have a disagreement over patients——'

'But Mrs Norris isn't your patient. If I'd come running to you complaining about Dr Higgins or suggesting that his judgment was anything less than perfect, you'd have laughed at me. Anyway, I'm not supposed to go round talking about patients' affairs. You'd have told me off for that, too,' she insisted.

Hal looked at her stubborn face, her pink cheeks and the firmness of righteous indignation in the angle of her chin and tried not to laugh with sheer pleasure at her. There was something about her, so solid and wholesome, so utterly reliable, that he knew all this was a storm in a teacup. Nevertheless, it was his duty to be stern.

'You're too good a nurse not to realise what you've done.' He sat down on the arm of the sofa and leaned over her. His face was serious and very handsome, Rosie thought, as he lectured her. 'You have made your relationship with Dr Higgins, and to a certain extent with me, very difficult because we both know now that if you disagree with us you may choose not to heed our diagnoses or advice —and that's very dangerous, Rosie. In this case it may appear to be black and white; it may eventually seem that you did the right thing. But you're not qualified and you're certainly not experienced enough to go over our heads for anything. And,' he added ruefully, stroking his chin where the first dark shadow of stubble was beginning to appear, 'you make things very difficult between Philip and me.'

'I can't see why.' Rosie studied her hands very closely, more shocked by his lack of approval than by anything else. As she'd picked up the phone and asked to be put through to Admissions at the hospital she'd been given confidence by a strong belief that Hal would have agreed with her had he been there. If she hadn't felt that way she wouldn't have done it. She *couldn't* have done it. To discover now that he would have disapproved was confusing. She'd refused to be browbeaten by Philip Higgins when he'd come storming in to demand what she'd done because she knew in her heart she was right; she knew Hal would think it was right.

But he didn't. She'd let him down again. She'd made a fool of herself again. She felt her heart sink and misery began to creep through her.

'Philip now thinks we're in cahoots. He is very keen to have things done properly. He's very traditional in his outlook and isn't keen on all the community and recreational facilities I intend to develop here.' Hal sighed. One of his legs, so slim and firm in their dark grey suiting, brushed hers as he sat on the arm of the sofa. Neither of them moved. 'I shouldn't be talking to you about a fellow colleague like this!' Hal leapt up at last and stood facing her, his eyes flashing. 'Damn it, Rosie, I end up saying to you things I'd never dream of saying to anyone else!' The smile that crinkled the tiny lines around his eyes took any sting from the words.

'When you took me on you said you wanted someone who wouldn't turn people away. You didn't want another Claire, you said. It's all very confusing.' Rosie shook her head.

'I don't want you turning people away. I want you to be just as you are, so that anyone can come to you and confide in you and tell you things that possibly they wouldn't tell me or Philip. But I don't think we can have you phoning up and taking over.' His eyes danced with a mischievous idea. 'Well, at least don't let on that you're calling officially. Go down to the box at the end of the road and call an ambulance and make it look like an accident.'

Rosie giggled. 'You're not serious!'

Hal inclined his head so that she still couldn't tell if he was joking or not. 'The ambulance will come and pick your casualty up and if they're ill they'll be admitted. And at least I won't have Philip Higgins breathing down my neck about insubordination!'

'It's all right, I won't do it again. And I won't start abusing the system, either,' Rosie promised.

'Good. This'll all blow over in the next few days, so don't get worried about it. And if Mrs Norris turns out to be suffering from anything we didn't know about, I'll make sure that Philip eats his words.' Hal watched the relief spread over Rosie's broad face. There was, despite all her problems in the last few hours, something sparkling about her —she had a gleam in her eye that he hadn't noticed before. Impulsively he reached out and squeezed her hand. Her fingers were very soft and warm. Her nails were short and neat, not like Claire's pink talons. He must remind her again to cut them. It didn't look professional and she might one day be called on to give emergency treatment and find them a hindrance.

'I'll see you tomorrow and we'll try to smooth it over with Philip.' His words were very quiet, almost whispered, and Rosie couldn't take her eyes off him.

How could she possibly *not* fall in love with such a man? It was quite impossible. Whatever he did, whatever he said, he was so good and kind . . . An inner warning sounded. Hadn't she thought that Mr Levete was so good and kind? Didn't she tend to fall hook line and sinker for any man who didn't behave like Genghis Khan? And yet none of them turned out to be as nice as they seemed. They all had a harsh word or a callous look when it came to it . . .

Someone banged briskly at the door downstairs and Hal got to his feet. 'That'll be Claire, I expect,' he said bashfully. 'I expect she wants a lift home. I'll go down and let myself out. Remember, Rosie, if you have anything you feel anxious about—well,' he amended, 'anything in the medical line that is—come and see me.'

Rosie took note of that little qualification. It meant one thing and one thing only. He suspected that she might feel more than just an employee's loyalty to him and he was warning her off. That last, throwaway barb stung deeply in her flesh, dissolving all the kind things he'd said earlier. Hadn't he talked about smoothing things over with Philip? Hadn't he sat firmly on the fence, agreeing for one minute that she was justified in doubting Philip's word and then the next minute telling her how wrong it was and that she mustn't do it again? The hypocrisy of the man! All he was doing was trying to stop any fuss, and while that was all he was concerned with, his patients might be allowed to suffer. He was just going to cover things up. And yet when he'd stooped in front of her and held her hand for a brief moment, she'd felt that there was nothing in the world she wouldn't do for him. Maybe *that* was what they meant by charisma. Or maybe he was just incredibly skilled at keeping people happy so that they would do the things he wanted them to do for him. Rosie's blood began a slow boil. Hal Dickinson was not what he seemed —and she had fallen for his act!

'Rosie's rather blotted her copybook, I hear.' Claire's voice bore no malicious overtones. She really didn't feel anything but mild interest and amusement in Rosie. 'I'm sorry to hear it. I've seen Mrs Norris in the surgery before now and felt that there really must be something terribly wrong with her, but Philip just put it down to premature senile dementia. He never seemed to take much notice. I think it was very brave of Rosie to go behind his back like that.'

'You do, do you?' Hal's voice expressed extreme cynicism. 'And when did you get your medical qualifications?' His mouth was compressed as he waited for a van to pull out in front of him, and he changed gear with a fierce slam of the wrist.

'There's no need to be like that.' Claire gazed ahead at the countryside just coming into its most beautiful leaf, and tried to stifle the tears that welled unasked in her eyes. When Hal was in this sort of mood there was no talking to him. He'd never been like this to her in the years she'd known him before she'd married Dick, but these days he barely had a good word to say for her. Even when they went out together he seemed strained, as if only half of him wanted to be in her company. For ten minutes he would be the most delightful companion—and then his mind would seem to wander; he'd look at her with a vagueness in his eyes, and for a while seem lost to her. It made her heart ache, but it also reminded her of what she'd done to him in the past, the way she'd hurt him. Sometimes she wondered if she would ever win him back. It was strange; three or four months ago she'd thought she was beginning to win and that he'd started to forgive her and fall in love with her all over again. And then something had happened, she wasn't sure what, and he was gradually becoming more distant again.

'You know Rosie's right,' she reprimanded him mildly. 'It's just a pity no one did what she's done months ago!'

'Don't try my patience, Claire. I've had enough

of this for one day.' Hal's hands tightened on the steering wheel and his knuckles whitened threateningly.

'*You've* had enough of it! And what about poor Rosie who's being torn to shreds from all sides? Philip wants her guts for garters and you're not going to do anything about it. I don't call that very fair.' Claire's voice was soft but firm. It rankled with Hal, reminding him of how little real support he'd given Rosie. He didn't want to hear any more criticism.

'If you don't drop the subject you can get out of the car and walk home,' he warned, trying to inject a jokey note into his voice.

'Just pull in here then.' Clare released her seat-belt and reached into the back of the car. 'Because I'm not going to keep quiet and say nothing just to make you feel better. Here, you can stop here.' She had her door open an inch as Hal, teeth gritted with an obstinate desire to test how far she would go, pulled into the side of the road. Surely she wouldn't get out and walk home? Perhaps she wanted him to apologise, to break down and say how much he loved her and wanted her . . . He knew, with a shudder, that he couldn't say it. In fact, he discovered, he didn't really care very much for her at all right now.

'Fine. You've only got a quarter of a mile to go from here.' His voice was clipped and betrayed no emotion except impatience. Claire climbed out without a word and slammed the door shut on him. And somehow, as it banged as he revved up and sped away, they both knew that whatever had been between them, it was over. It was as if, in her show of support for Rosie and her sudden spark of independence, Claire had freed herself of something that had been dogging her. And as Hal watched her slim figure recede into the distance in his rearview mirror he felt nothing but a curious relief. There had been no major row; no big ultimatum that if he loved her he would marry her. It had ended quite simply and without great fuss on a country road.

'Have you heard the news?' Mrs Hammond came quietly into the common room and made Rosie, who was just boiling the kettle for some coffee, jump. For a moment she thought that it might be Philip Higgins back early from his visits, and she was doing her very best to avoid him. And he was obviously trying to do the same with her, for he'd not sent a patient to her for nearly three days.

'No. What's happened now?' Rosie was beginning to feel wary about news. She had a faint suspicion that her action the other day had stirred up a whole can of worms. Hal had looked thunderous when she'd seen him and Claire had been pale and strained behind the reception screen. Something was afoot, she knew, and she had a suspicion that it might involve her resignation. At first, after Hal had been to see her she had just seethed with rage at his attitude. But since then she'd begun to realise the true magnitude of her behaviour—and surely, if Philip's honour was to be satisfied, her sacking or resignation would be required.

'Claire's leaving. She handed in her notice this morning.' Mrs Hammond did not look displeased, as one might have expected of a woman who had just lost her assistant.

'What's she going to do?' Rosie poured water

into two mugs, dunked the coffee bags firmly, and handed one to Mrs Hammond, hoping that her suddenly shaky hands would not betray her.

'I don't think she knows herself—says she'll go back to London and see what she can get there.' Mrs Hammond's eyes twinkled. 'I must say, I thought she had more spirit; if she'd stayed around long enough he'd have *had* to marry her, he's that sort of man. But something must have happened between them.'

'Will you be able to find yourself a replacement?' Rosie asked warily, refusing to be drawn into gossip and speculation, yet feeling relief all the same. Mrs Hammond knew so much; she seemed to absorb information from the atmosphere. Perhaps she knew what Rosie's fate was to be.

'There's that nice girl, Tracy Marchbank. She's very bright and willing and she's worked for the dentist in Woodbridge, so she knows how to deal with people. I've had my eye on her for some time.'

Mrs Hammond raised an eyebrow at Rosie's surprised look. 'Oh, this has been coming for some time now. Claire's a nice enough girl but she's not cut out for keeping a caring watch over people. She's had a difficult life in the past year or two and naturally she needs to spend time thinking about herself and taking care of her life. You know yourself, Rosie, that if you're going to do something properly here you've got to give yourself to it one hundred per cent. This job has been a sort of therapy for Claire, and that's probably why Dr Dickinson brought her here in the first place.'

Rosie absorbed the information as calmly as she could, but her heart could not be prevented from beating just a little faster and a strange feeling of elation could not be stopped from slipping over her. Not that this meant anything about the way Hal felt towards *her*, of course. But Claire, while never rude or less than pleasant to her face, always made Rosie feel nervous—and part of that nervousness was Rosie's unshaken belief that Claire was central to Hal's life. And now, quite suddenly, she wasn't.

'You're looking very tired, my dear,' Mrs Hammond observed, pouring herself some more coffee. 'Has this thing with Mrs Guthrie been getting you down?'

'I don't know what it is,' Rosie admitted, yawning. 'I can't seem to find any energy. I haven't been sleeping too well recently, but it's not just that. I feel so . . .'

'It's to be understood.' The older woman leant across the table and patted Rosie's arm. 'You're in a new job and you've been working hard to get all these new projects and ideas off the ground. It's natural that you'll come to the end of your natural enthusiasm after a while. Tell me,' she asked with a hint of mischief in her eyes, 'are you happy here? Now that all the excitement's settled down and it's becoming just hard work, are you still enjoying it?'

'Oh yes!' Quite where the emphatic answer came from, Rosie wasn't sure, because all in all the last week or two hadn't been exactly the best time she'd had in her life. But there was no doubt about it; something made Clayburgh and the clinic special. And she knew, without having to think too hard, just what—or more accurately *who*—that something was. Life here without Hal Dickinson was almost impossible to imagine. If he were to go, she didn't think that she could have said yes with such certainty. And yet it was ridiculous to base one's happiness on a complete fantasy; it was quite mad to live from day to day for the smile of a man who didn't really give two hoots about her.

Rosie dropped her mug on the table with a loud clunk. She had done it again, she realised with shame—she had fallen for a colleague. All these weeks she had been kidding herself that what she felt for that was just admiration, a shared aim and belief in looking after people. But now, with Claire out of the way, she could see her feelings for what they really were.

'Tell me,' she asked Mrs Hammond quietly, 'am I in awful trouble about Mrs Norris?'

Mrs Hammond tilted back her grey head and laughed. 'Trouble? Of a sort, I suppose. You've stirred up a hornet's nest, that's what you've done my dear, though I suspect we'll soon all be grateful for it.'

'But all I . . .'

Mrs Hammond silenced her with an admonitory finger, took a sneaking glance at the door to check that no one else had entered, and then bent her head conspiratorially to Rosie. 'I expect you've noticed that Hal Dickinson and Philip Higgins are not, as one might say, bosom friends?'

'Well . . .'

'They're not, I assure you,' Mrs Hammond sighed. 'When Philip joined the practice he was full of bright ideas about developing things. He talked about being stifled in London, how wonderful it would be to get out into the countryside—and no doubt he meant it sincerely at the time. But he's really a town bird. You must know that he goes back to London most weekends.'

Rosie nodded non-commitally. She didn't really have much idea of what Philip Higgins got up to in his spare time.

'And you know that he insists on using a deputising service instead of doing his share of on-calls?' Rosie shook her head. 'Well you do now—and you'll understand why Dr Dickinson is less than happy about the situation. They had a huge row about this Guthrie and Norris thing, so maybe it won't be long before Dr Higgins decides that Clayburgh isn't the right place for him, like Claire.'

'But this is terrible!' Rosie cried. 'The moment I arrive everyone else begins to leave!'

'Don't exaggerate,' Mrs Hammond said warmly as she rose from the table and went to wash her mug. 'We all knew that Claire wasn't going to stay—unless it was in some other capacity. And everyone here knew within three weeks of Dr Higgins' arrival that his heart wasn't really involved. Things began to look up, I must say though, when you arrived. I think by that time Hal was beginning to despair of finding anyone who'd feel the same way about the place as we do. I hope he wasn't too hard on you over Mrs Guthrie?'

'Well . . .' Rosie could feel a warm flush of pleasure at these generous words stealing over her. She had sensed that everything was not roses between Hal and Philip, but she hadn't been sure what it was. Now she began to see the light.

'I shall have a word with him,' Mrs Hammond said firmly, snatching Rosie's mug up. 'I think he's rather neglected you since you arrived—but then when someone takes over and does as well as you've been doing, perhaps the tendency is to leave them alone. Well, I shall insist that you have a bit of a break and I'll point out to him how hard you're working.'

Rosie jumped up in alarm. 'Please, don't! Honestly, he's been very nice. I wasn't so worried that I . . .'

'I know you don't want me to make a fuss, and I won't. But I think that if anything has been said to make you feel unhappy or insecure then he ought to correct the impression,' Mrs Hammond insisted. 'And now I've got to get back to the desk for the ante-natal clinic—and you should be getting ready to do the weights and measures.'

And with that businesslike reminder, Mrs Hammond went on her way. Rosie didn't know whether to sink into the ground with embarrassment at the thought of what she might say to Hal, or to bask in the pleasure of the compliments that had come her way. She hoped with all her heart that Mrs Hammond wouldn't make any fuss.

Ante-natal mornings were fun. One of the community midwives came in for them, and they were always good-humoured and amusing. In fact, Rosie reflected as she assisted with an internal examination, working with the midwives was rather like assisting in an outpatient clinic in a hospital. She may not have been at Clayburgh very long, but she'd got into the habit of thinking and doing things by herself, and it was quite a novelty to stand quietly by, handing instruments and swabs to someone else!

'Hmmm . . .' Libby Benjamin, who was a short lady in her early forties with curly hair and a kindly smile, snapped off her gloves. 'Lovely, Mrs Preece. I think we'll bring that date forward by a few days, though. Either it's going to be a particularly large

baby or it's due on the . . .' She took the chart from
Rosie, counted quickly on her fingers and
announced, 'I'd say it's likely to make its appearance on the fourteenth. How's that? We'll get
Doctor to check, of course.'

'That'll be all right,' Mrs Preece said after a
moment of studied thought. 'In fact if it arrives on
the fourteenth it'll be a Cancer and not a Gemini.
My husband's a Gemini, Nurse,' she explained with
a self-mocking grin, 'and he can be very difficult to
cope with at times.'

'Funny how some people put so much emphasis
on the birth date,' Midwife Benjamin reflected
later as they sat together finishing up the files and
making notes on who hadn't managed to come and
would need to be seen later in the week. 'Especially
when you consider how haphazard a system we
have for predicting the arrival of the baby and all
the modern developments, like induction, that
can bring it into the world before it is quite ready.
Take my third daughter—now she was due in
September, which means that she should have been
a Virgo, but she was a good three weeks' premature
because of a problem I had, so she ended up
officially a Leo. And she doesn't fit either of those
star signs,' she chuckled as she did up her briefcase.
'Which only goes to show that one shouldn't judge
people by anything except their actions—not their
date of birth, their looks, or anything else. Simply
by what they say and do.'

With a few more instructions about where to find
her and when she would next call at the health
centre, she went off to check with the health visitors
who were having a lunchtime meeting.

Rosie tidied the surgery and then went up to her

own flat for some lunch. With any luck she might be able to take a nap for a few hours, she thought wearily as she climbed the stairs. She felt as if she could sleep for a week; it had been as much as she could do to restrain herself from yawning over Mrs Preece. Nothing she did seemed to make her feel any better—neither a few hours extra in bed in the form of an early night nor countless cups of coffee to give her more energy. Not even a thickly chocolate-covered candy bar had given her more go. Perhaps, she thought as she sank into the comfort of the sofa with some bread and cheese to hand on the coffee table, it was the emotional stress and strain she had been under recently. Although she'd been through many a sticky patch in her life before . . . With that thought still in her head, Rosie fell asleep.

CHAPTER EIGHT

'THERE you are. Come back and see me again on Friday and I'll dress it for you.' Rosie ushered the patient, who had come in to have an anti-tetanus jab for a deep cat bite, out of the door. The poor woman was still in a state of shock, for apparently her cat had never so much as scratched her before in its life, and now it had ruined its reputation by biting almost through one of her fingertips. Rosie hoped that it would be all right. It had seemed clean enough and she didn't want to approach either doctor at the moment for an antibiotic. Before calling in the next patient she shut the surgery door and went to the basin, where she drew herself a long drink of cold water. Quite what was wrong with her she didn't know, but her thirst seemed unquenchable. It wasn't even as if it was hot, she mused as she downed the glassful and filled it again. Perhaps she was sickening for something; flu or a throat infection, maybe. They both made people feel thirsty. Wiping her mouth, she went out to the waiting area.

There were no patients left, but Hal was standing there. The very sight of him gave Rosie a sudden burst of energy. It was as if the air were suddenly pure oxygen, sending deep, relieving pulses of life into her veins and lungs.

It was two days since she had last seen him, and in that time he seemed to have changed. Not physically. He was still as upright and rangy and dizzyingly good-looking as he had been. But in his face something had changed. A line of tension that hadn't been there before had appeared across his brow. Of course; he had only just split up with Claire. He would be bound to feel some kind of strain.

He sat on the edge of the desk, casually dressed today in well-washed black cords that had faded to a subtle charcoal colour and a slubby blue and grey pullover with a restrained Fair Isle design. His hands on the desk were only inches from her own, and they were already slightly tanned, she noticed. He must have been out sailing again and caught what sunshine there had been. As if in a dream she watched her own fingers stretch out towards them, as if she would touch him—but at the last moment she pulled them back. No matter how much she liked being with him, looking at him, thinking about him, when she was actually at his side she felt nothing but inadequacy. He was so good-looking, so unattainable; she felt embarrassment at even daring to imagine what it would be like to be with him for the rest of her life—to be his lover.

Unaccountably, he reached out and took her fingers, just as she'd been longing to take his. 'I wanted to ask you if you'd like to come and have a drink this evening. I've got to go on a call in a few minutes, but how would it be if I picked you up in about half an hour?' His eyes, normally so coolly navy that she didn't know what to read in them, seemed lighter tonight, and friendly. In her ears Rosie heard the echo of Mrs Hammond's words about getting him to be nice to her and swallowed down the initial lurch of excitement that had risen in her throat.

'That would be nice—if you're sure it wouldn't be inconvenient,' she added.

'Not at all inconvenient. In fact I hope to have some news for you.' Hal rose to go. He wanted to make a larger gesture, perhaps to kiss her or hug her, though when he looked at her he wondered quite why this magic had overcome him. She was no beauty. She simply radiated warmth and good nature and kindness, and there was, deep in her too, a hidden strength that attracted something in him. For two days now he had kept away, almost frightened that now Claire was going he would have no defence against whatever it was that had made him lose his head in this way. Didn't they say that love is blind? Hal shook his head disbelievingly as he walked away down the corridor. He certainly wasn't blind to Rosie's faults. He wasn't in love.

'You're sure that this isn't inconvenient?' Rosie could have bitten off her tongue for allowing such stupid words to pass her lips. She was just inviting him to make an excuse and leave her—for, after all, this was only a courtesy suggested by Mrs Hammond. Despite the loss of Claire, Hal could probably think of a hundred and one better things to do with his evening.

'We wouldn't be going out if it were. But you'll have to forgive me if my bleeper goes and I have to take off to a call,' he smiled, touched by her lack of confidence in herself. 'I thought we'd get out of Clayburgh for a bit. You can't have seen a great deal of the countryside and I know a good pub over towards Melton.'

'It sounds lovely.' Rosie hoped he didn't feel the shudder that went through her as his hand in the small of her back ushered her firmly to the car in the parking space outside the clinic. At the same time, with the ingrown suspicion that as far as a girl like her was concerned, nothing could ever be simple, she wondered whether he was taking her for a drink out of town so as to avoid being seen locally with her. No matter what he said or did, the suspicion burned.

Hal got in beside her and they turned down the main street and out of Clayburgh. He obviously knew exactly where he was going, so perhaps this Melton pub was a regular haunt. Perhaps he wasn't just trying to hide her away. 'Now for that news I told you about,' he announced calmly as he steered around the tight bends in the road. 'I've been to have a chat with the geriatrician from Woodbridge. They're keeping Mrs Norris in for investigation. They can't be exactly sure of what she's suffering from until some tests have been done, but they're worried enough about her to keep her in. George Howe—he's the specialist—told me to congratulate you on taking action. He says that as far as he's concerned too many people put down treatable illness to some inevitable process of ageing. And I have to echo his thoughts. Well done, Rosie. I'm only sorry that you caught so much flack.'

He turned to her briefly as he finished and gave her an encouragingly warm smile, catching in return the rewarding glint of happiness and relief in her dark eyes. She was such a natural person; she seemed incapable of putting on an act. Hal breathed deeply and concentrated on the road. He could feel what he fondly thought of as his better judgment slipping away by the minute.

'That's going to make life even more difficult

with Dr Higgins,' Rosie thought aloud. 'At least if I'd been wrong his honour would have been avenged. And we were beginning to work together so well. Now he's going to find it impossible to work with me.'

Hal gave a conspiratorial laugh and indicated a right turn. 'That's rather what I hope.'

Rosie digested this comment for a moment while the car pulled up into the car-park of a beamed, typically Suffolk pink-washed pub, with a thatched roof. What did this last cryptic comment mean? Mrs Hammond's words of praise for her work echoed at the back of her mind, but she didn't have the confidence in herself to believe that Hal might want to lose Philip and retain herself. Hal watched her face as she got out and slammed the car door.

'What I should have said,' he murmured as he guided her into the bar, 'was that the clinic would be a better place without Philip. I was *not* inviting you to do the decent thing and hand in your resignation.' He laughed. 'I don't know how we ever managed without you, and apart from an initial burst of enthusiasm when he first arrived, the place hasn't benefited much from Philip's presence. And now we've got that sorted out, what would you like to eat and drink?'

The pub was low-beamed and cosy inside, with slate floors and an inglenook fireplace full of baskets packed with dried flowers and herbs. A few people stood at the bar and a few more sat eating at tables in the windows. Rosie ordered a long glass of cold cider and went to sit down and peruse the menu. It offered such homely delights as shepherd's pie and steak and kidney pudding, but also a few more adventurous dishes.

'I can recommend the fish,' Hal said as he set down the glasses. 'The man who runs this place has good contacts. And he's a sailor—and I've never met a sailor who doesn't appreciate good fish.'

They both laughed and sipped their drinks, and in a few minutes the last of the tension between them seemed to have evaporated. They chatted about work matters, careful not to mention names or specific cases, lest anyone be eavesdropping. Hal talked about Caroline the cow and how her calf was doing, and Rosie told stories of her days at Highstead and her childhood down in Devon.

'I think that's some of the loveliest countryside on earth,' Hal mused. 'Exmoor, all those wonderful green hills rolling into the sea . . . Not that Suffolk's a bad place to live,' he added quickly. 'I'd hate to think any of the locals could hear me praising another spot. They all think that Suffolk is the most wonderful place in the world.'

'It's not bad,' Rosie giggled, downing the last of her second glass of cider. 'Do you think I could have a glass of water? I've got a raging thirst. I can't seem to get enough to drink these days.'

Hal looked at her questioningly. 'When did this start?' he enquired casually, but there was something in his manner that alerted Rosie. It was suddenly as if she was in the consulting room.

'Four or five days ago. A week, maybe. It didn't seem so bad at first and I just thought that I had a throat infection starting. Why?' She looked up at him almost nervously. In the back of her mind she'd known that it was not something to be ignored, but she didn't feel inclined to investigate the cause.

'Nothing,' he shrugged lightly. 'I'm a GP,

remember, and you excited my professional curiosity for a moment!' Yet his smile as he returned to the bar was not as relaxed as it had been.

'They always say that doctors and nurses are the worst people in the world for looking after their health,' Rosie joked when he placed a glass and a jug of iced water on the table.

'Well I can't afford to have *you* going off sick,' was his distracted reply. They ate their halibut in silence. It was delicious, and even more delicious was the quiet comfort that existed between them. Rosie couldn't remember ever feeling so relaxed in a man's company before—but then, she supposed, she'd never drunk quite so much cider quite so quickly before, and alcohol probably had something to do with it.

She looked up from her plate to find Hal watching her closely. And for once her immediate reaction wasn't one of remorse that she didn't look better, but sheer pleasure in having his attention. 'You know, you have such lovely glowing skin,' he said quietly, almost to himself.

'Thank you.' Rosie tried to swallow the food in her mouth but felt it stick in her dry throat. Wasn't that the kind of compliment men always paid to women who had no better points to remark on? If she'd had a lovely figure or face he might have said as much. If she'd been elegant or had long, slim hands he'd have fixed on that. But a lovely skin . . . It had to be the most backhanded compliment of all time.

'It was a very nice try at a compliment, Hal, but simply because Mrs Hammond told you to be nice to me doesn't mean you have to bring me out and pay me compliments.' She listened to her words and then added shamefacedly, 'I'm sorry. I've ruined it all now. And we were having such a nice time.'

'What's wrong? Why can't you believe that I'm sincere?' Hal took her hand across the table and felt certain that he could see the sparkle of a tear in her eye. 'Rosie, I meant it. You're a lovely girl and you honestly do have remarkable skin. You're not covered in make-up like most women. I like it that way. I hate to see girls covered in the stuff.' He sighed, but he did not let go of her hand. 'What's wrong? Has no one ever paid you a compliment before?'

'No. Well, not really. No one who wasn't old enough to be my grandfather.' Rosie managed the ghost of a smile and felt the heat of his fingers against hers. She didn't know what to think about what was going on. If he should really mean what he said, if he should really feel something more than friendship for her . . . Panic welled up in her. All she'd thought and dreamed about the past few weeks would be a nightmare if it actually happened. How would she cope with his feelings, with hers?

'I can't possibly think why.' Hal's eyes were dark and sensual across the table. 'What's happened to drain you of your confidence, Rosie? You don't seem to realise how much other people like and admire you, or how strongly they feel towards you. And you should know better than to think I've brought you here because of Mrs Hammond. I haven't had time to talk to her today, but indispensable as she is, I don't take too much notice of her reports and gossip.'

'I'm sorry.' Rosie regarded her plate in silence.

'I'm not very graceful when it comes to accepting compliments.'

'Well you can start to practise being graceful now, Nurse Simpson, because I'm going to shower you with them.' Hal felt a sudden spurt of exhilaration. Paying compliments was something he normally did without a great deal of thought. Claire and the various other women he'd been involved with seemed to expect them as a matter of course and accepted them without this delightful show of modesty. He'd become stale and insincere. But now he wanted to please Rosie, to restore in her some of the self-esteem that seemed to have been knocked out of her. With wounding remorse, he remembered the night that Claire had been so rude about her and the pain in Rosie's dark eyes as she had tried to hide from them. No wonder she couldn't accept praise. Who knows how many times she has been hurt like that in the past, he wondered to himself.

'First, in your capacity as Nurse Simpson you have been tolerant, quick to learn, wonderfully sympathetic to our patients, and full of good ideas for the clinic. In fact you've done more for the place than I could ever have asked or expected. And I haven't done nearly enough to thank you for it,' he said quietly but with such firmness that Rosie could only listen and absorb and believe that what he said was what he felt. 'And in your capacity as Rosie Simpson you have been generous and kind when I could least have asked for kindness. You have been a delightful companion. You've strengthened my beliefs about the clinic and its future and my kind of medicine at every turn. And what's more, on top of all that, and nowhere near as important, comes the fact that you have a lovely skin, and beautiful eyes, soft hands and a charming voice. Your problem is, Rosie, that you're simply too kind and gentle for your own good. One of these days someone will come along and take advantage of you.'

His fingers brushed the inside of her wrist as he spoke, sending small shivers of response through her. And she couldn't stop the tears rising in her eyes at his words. 'Is that the nicest thing anyone has ever said to you?' he asked gently, bending across the table to shield her from the interested looks of the couple nearby.

'Yes,' Rosie sniffed, distrusting the happiness that crowded in her, lest he should turn out to have been joking after all. People could be so cruel. Once or twice in her youth a handsome lad had flirted with her merely as a joke, waiting for her quick response and then throwing it back in her face with a jeering, 'You didn't think I was really interested in *you*!' Her natural self-defences stopped her from trusting anyone—particularly after Giles Levete.

'Good. Because conceited as it may sound, I want to be the person who has said the nicest things ever to you. Rosie, I . . .' The words stuck in his throat. The words that had come so easily for other women, which had tripped off his tongue without a second's hesitation, wouldn't come now when he felt so much like saying them. 'Rosie,' he stumbled, 'I think we'd better go.'

Rosie was so stunned by what he had said that she didn't hear the faint pause, the sudden reversal of tone. She got to her feet without reluctance. 'It's been lovely,' she smiled, still aware of the tears on her eyelashes. 'But I like to be in bed as early as possible these days.'

With someone more sophisticated Hal might have picked up the double entendre and made a joke out of it. Instead he just paid the bill and led her out. His own mind was in uproar. What had he nearly said? That he was beginning to fall in love with her? What folly had he been about to commit? God or an angel must have been hanging around at that particular moment to shut him up so fortuitously.

'How long have you been feeling so tired?' he asked absent-mindedly as they got back into the car.

'Oh, a fortnight or so. I don't know what it is. Probably some bug. It's not so much feeling tired as just being totally without energy. Sometimes in the evening I can hardly drag myself back up the stairs to the flat. I even fell asleep once and woke up at four in the morning in the sitting-room with the radio blaring at me.' She looked out at the dark shapes of trees and bushes speeding by, the occasional house with its windows lit up. Long ago she had persuaded herself to accept that a nice cosy house with a husband and children and a comfortable life were out of the question for her. There were some women who had to earn their living all their lives; women who would always come home to an empty house. Now, for the first time for ages, she began to wonder if she dared hope. 'Thank you for this evening,' she began nervously. 'It's really meant a lot to me.'

Hal didn't seem to hear her for a few seconds. Then he spoke suddenly. 'Before you go back to the flat, I want you to come into the surgery with me. I want to take a blood test.'

'What for?' It was such a ludicrous suggestion that she laughed.

'I'm surprised that someone who's so informed about Huntington's chorea doesn't know the two major symptoms of diabetes,' was his grim reply.

'There, that didn't hurt, did it?' Hal held up the syringe of blood, almost black in the artificial light, and grinned ironically. 'Sorry, Rosie. I say that to all my patients.' He turned to the trolley which was kept loaded and supplied for his needs, searching for a sample bottle to transfer the blood to. 'Damn it. I'll have to come along to your surgery. I'm out of samples.'

'Just a second.' Rosie went to button the wrist-band of her cuff. She was still shocked, both by the idea that she might have developed diabetes and the touch of Hal's firm but gentle fingers on her arm.

'Hold on. I haven't even given you a plaster. A fine doctor I am.' He laughed to lighten the atmosphere, and bent to stick a small plaster over the puncture. It wasn't even bleeding. On impulse he lowered his mouth and kissed the inside of her elbow with tender care, once, twice . . . he lost count until he felt her fingers in his hair and he raised his head to kiss her gently on the lips. At first she didn't respond and he knew that her defences and her natural distrust of him were holding her back. And then, unable to prevent herself, her lips quickened and her arms rose to hold him. He was so firm, so solid. Her hands ran, marvelling, over his back and shoulders as his teeth nipped her ear and his tongue discovered the softness of her neck.

She had never held a man so close, never known anything like this. It was like discovering a new universe; like finding there was a whole range of sensation she had missed. Instinctively she kissed him, and with a sigh he kissed her more tenderly. A flame of delight began to flicker in them both. Rosie felt every inch of her body beginning to pulse with something new, something unknown as he held her and kissed her again and again. But what if, a tiny voice at the very back of her mind asked, he's only having you on? And how will you be able to face each other tomorrow if this gets out of hand? And anyway, what do you know about love? You've no experience, you don't even know what to do. How can you possibly hope to make him happy?

'Hal, don't. Please.' Rosie's eyes, reproachful and swimming with tears, looked down on him. 'I don't think this is a good idea.'

She saw the pulse in his jaw beginning to subside, and smoothed back his ruffled hair. He cleared his throat before he spoke, but his voice still caught scratchily. 'Yes, you're absolutely right. This is not a good idea.' He stood up, and she felt him embarrassed, angry with himself and with her. He had made a fool of himself. He had practically forced himself on her, and although she had responded at first, it was probably only in surprise at his behaviour.

'I'm sorry, Rosie. I didn't mean that to happen.' He turned away to pick up the syringe he'd left in a kidney bowl, and without another word left the room to find a suitable sample bottle for it.

Before he could return, before they were forced to stand awkwardly in the surgery and talk like embarrassed strangers, Rosie picked up her bag and hurried out, round the front of the building and up into the sanctuary of her flat. Her mind reeled and her body ached for his touch—and yet she did not know what to make of what had just happened. All the signs were that he was attracted to her, that he liked her and wanted her. But what was to be made of his words? He'd said just now that none of it should have happened. And surely the last thing a man like him could want was an affair with a plump nurse? And on top of that he suspected, and she knew with hideous certainty, there was diabetes . . .

She got ready for bed slowly, pausing silently now and then to listen to the rattle of the keys as he locked the doors, the slam of his car door as he climbed in, and the roar of the engine. He was not going to come after her. He knew as well as she did that the way things were at the moment they could never trust each other. Something in her would not allow her to trust him with her happiness. And that was probably a good thing, she decided as she wearily climbed into bed. They said, she mused in the darkness, that love could conquer all. But there was one thing it couldn't conquer, and that was her instinctive feeling that no man, not even Hal Dickinson, could love her. And not even all the compliments in the world, not even all the care and tenderness, was enough to break that barrier down.

CHAPTER NINE

'COME in, Rosie.' Hal stood silhouetted against the window of his room, one hand in the pocket of his pale grey trousers, the other holding a small sheet of paper which Rosie recognised only too well as a lab report. He looked tired, as if he hadn't been sleeping well. Rosie paused before coming forward into the room. It was almost impossible to look at him, for just the sight of him reminded her of what had happened here, in this very room, only three nights ago. Since then she'd managed to keep out of his way and he had avoided bumping into her. They had talked briefly on the telephone when he called to say that he was sending a patient to her, and he had been briefly friendly, but nothing had been said about what had happened.

'It's bad news, I'm afraid.' He pulled the chair out from the desk, so that he was not sitting behind it and dominating her, and motioned her to sit down. 'The lab report confirms what I expected. Your insulin mechanism has started to break down and your blood sugar level is getting dangerously high.' He paused and watched her. It hurt him to pronounce such a diagnosis. It cut him to the quick to see her, so fresh and vulnerable and being done down again by life. 'Technically you're diabetic.'

'Am I going to have to have insulin injections?' she asked calmly. In the intervening three days there had been time enough to read up about the disease and prepare herself for it. Indeed, she had already cleared out the kitchen and changed her diet. From now on there would be no chocolate or sweets, none of the things she'd fallen back on when things had gone wrong in the past. And strangely enough it felt good to know that she could help herself in this way. Not that she hadn't tried dieting before, but it hadn't seemed a matter of life and death then. Now it really would be important, and she would have to set an example to the three or four local diabetics who came in to have their progress checked.

'No, thank goodness. We've caught it in time. It should just be a matter of diet. Lots of diabetics find that they're nearly cured by some simple changes to their diet, and I hope you'll be one of them. And I'm here to keep a close eye on you.' His smile was so sympathetic, so tender, that she couldn't help but smile back.

'That's nice to know,' she responded quietly. 'And it will mean that I can still drive and work. Having to have injections might have made things more difficult.'

'There are loads of people who have to inject themselves. Famous actors and politicians and people in all walks of life, and all of them living just about as normally as the rest of the population, so don't go getting sorry for yourself, Rosie. You can carry on here with no problems at all.' He frowned for a moment. 'Well, we might have to change your surgery times so that you can be sure of eating regularly, but that won't matter. Now,' he took up a card, 'I've arranged for you to go into Ipswich for a check-up. I didn't think you'd want somebody here in charge of the case, and you'd have to go there anyway to get the details of your diet worked out. They'll see you tomorrow morning.'

Rosie held up her hand. 'I can't, I'm doing an ante-natal exercise class and then some of the play-group trainees are coming round to organise something for the under-fives.'

'Claire can do that. I insist that you go along and see the specialist.' For the first time since their row about Mrs Norris, he seemed angry. 'The longer this is left, the worse the problem will become and the more you'll suffer. We should have spotted this when it first started. It was just luck that we went out and . . .' He faltered. He'd done nothing since that night but dwell on the scene and what it meant. All he knew was that this latest complication made him feel even more strongly about her than he had before, though God only knew why. Never before had he derived such pleasure from being with someone. Never before had he wanted so badly to please a woman, make her happy. Never before, except perhaps that first time round with Claire, had he felt so strongly that he wanted to share all he had and all he would ever have. And still he couldn't trust such unlikely feelings; still he could barely believe that his affections had alighted on and become firmly stuck to Rosie. Though each time they met, each time he spoke to her, each time he thought of her, and that was almost twenty-four hours a day, that distrust was breaking down.

'If you won't go into Ipswich on your own,' he threatened mockingly, 'I'll damn well put you in the car and take you over there myself.'

Rosie grinned and took note of the time of her appointment. Never had such bad medical news been shaken off so lightly. 'It's all right. I'll go on my own. But now I have to get the supply sheets prepared for the end of the week.' She left Hal in his surgery. His concern touched and pleased her. Perhaps it would be better if their relationship remained as one of caring friendship. Perhaps this was, anyway, where it had come to a halt. They must have had too much to drink the other night and been carried away by the situation. That was all, and that was all there could ever be between them.

Funny how hospitals always smelled the same! It was some time since she'd been in one—months, Rosie thought with surprise—and yet that familiar antiseptic smell immediately took her back to memories of Highstead. Once a nurse, always a nurse, she thought ruefully as she checked in at the reception desk and made her way through to the clinic she'd been instructed to attend. Fortunately her appointment was quite late in the morning and there weren't too many people ahead of her. She stifled her nerves, pretended to read a four-year-old edition of *Country Life*, and tried not to eavesdrop on the confidential medical details that could just be heard emanating from the consulting room. That was the trouble with being a nurse—you could understand what a doctor said when he mentioned all these technical terms!

Then her name was called and Rosie entered the inner sanctum wondering why, after all her experience, she felt so apprehensive. The examination was over quickly; so was a brief recounting of her blood tests and symptoms. She wasn't very keen on Dr Hillyard; he was obviously a man of the old school who wasn't too pleased at the realisation that his patient was so well-informed about her illness, and his manner was abrupt and, as she discovered, insensitive.

'Now, Nurse Simpson,' he said in a tone of voice which indicated his boredom with the case, 'how do you think you'll manage on this diet we've worked out? You're going to have to lose as much weight as possible in a short period. From looking at you I would say that your diet hasn't been controlled recently. And Dr Dickinson in his letter indicates that as far as he's concerned you're a compulsive eater . . .'

'I don't think I am,' Rosie interjected, shocked at this diagnosis. To be diabetic was one thing, but to be put down as a compulsive personality, to have it suggested that she wasn't in control of her life . . . Her personal feelings overcame her professional ones. How could Hal write down something like that? A hollow pain echoed inside her.

'Nurse Simpson, I hope I'm not going to hear excuses about you being big-boned, or hardly eating a thing, or having a difficult metabolism,' Dr Hillyard went on without interest. 'You're overweight because you've been eating too much, and that's the long and the short of it. Now what I want to know is whether you're going to want some extra help to cope with this diet—because if you start running to the biscuit tin with your condition you'll be asking for trouble.'

It was true, Rosie knew, but it hadn't been put to her in the most pleasant or diplomatic of ways. She felt embarrassment creeping over her. What did everyone think she was? A complete fool? Neurotic, perhaps? Maybe she had used food as a buffer against the world in the past. Maybe it *had* been a form of protection, guaranteed to safeguard her against the cunning ways of men who won a girl's heart only to let her down.

'What sort of professional help do you mean?' she replied absently, her mind sifting over some uncomfortable moments in her life. If she were thin and desirable, would she still find it hard to respond to Hal's touch? Was she just using the fact that she couldn't believe anyone as good-looking and kind as him would want *her*, as an excuse for not getting involved?

'We've got a little group of people such as yourself here—people with eating problems. It's overseen by a psychologist. . . .' Dr Hillyard went on to detail the various options open, but Rosie hardly heard a word he was saying. All she could feel was acute distress at the thought that Hal had diagnosed her as needing psychiatric help. And yet he had never said anything to her, never suggested anything. Perhaps he was just being kind, pretending that there was nothing wrong, just as one might to someone who was slightly crippled or had a terrible squint. Ignore the squint or the limp if you could, and show your sympathy and pity with a few kisses, a friendly evening out. And what was he thinking of her while they were out? *Poor girl*, maybe. *The poor girl doesn't have a boy-friend so I'll take her out and be nice to her. No one else does*. Was that why he had asked her out the other evening? The ideas fought within her, colliding, confusing, and refusing to be calmed. Cool thought and analysis were submerged beneath a whirlpool of conflicting emotions.

'I'll think about it and let you know,' Rosie heard herself saying to the doctor; then she was out of the consulting room and making an appointment to come back in two weeks' time, and then at last she was out in the fresh air. The breeze revived her as she stood on the steps and caught her breath. As a nurse she'd seen patients flee in this state and she'd always assumed that they'd just been told bad news. But what news could be worse than the realisation that the man you'd fallen in love with, the man who made your days bright and your work a delight, *pitied* you, Rosie thought as she stood there and pulled her jacket around her tightly. It was wrong to blame him—and yet who else was there to blame for the pain that eddied inside her? If he hadn't put up this sham of affection she wouldn't have fallen for him. He needn't have felt sorry for her, above all things!

'Rosie, there you are. I saw you tearing through Outpatients like a bat out of hell. Was everything all right?' Hal emerged through the swing doors as if Rosie's thoughts had summoned him. He was tall and vibrant in his washed faded jeans and a casual cream cotton sweater, the sleeves of which were pushed up high above his tanned wrists. He looked so outrageously masculine and full of health that she could have wept.

'What's wrong?' He noticed the tension in her face, the startled way in which she seemed to glance at him and then glance away, as if the sight of him hurt her. 'What did Hillyard say?'

'He said too much—but I'm very glad that he did, because now I begin to understand what's been going on.' Rosie walked down the steps in front of him and tugged her arm from his grasp as he tried to take it. She could feel him with her, hear his quiet footsteps as they came down the steps, but she couldn't look at him for fear of what she'd see on his face.

'What does that mean?' His voice was calm and like honey to her ears, but the bitterness of her thoughts cut through her instinctive reaction, which was to turn to him for comfort. 'Tell me, Rosie, is everything all right?'

Rosie could see the green bus that would take her back to Clayburgh pulling into the stop at the end of the hospital drive. It would be there for four minutes, no longer—she had worked it out on the timetable. She walked purposefully towards it, and Hal followed stride for stride, trying to watch her face but being studiously ignored.

'Yes, everything's all right, thank you,' she informed him briskly. 'Just a strict diet, which should stabilise the condition nicely. There's no need for too much concern. And he put me right on a couple of other things I needed to know about too, so now everything's going to be fine.'

'Good.' Hal's hand came down gently on the back of her neck and his fingers seemed to bring immediate comfort. 'I've got the car parked over here.' He gestured towards the small doctors' car-park at the end of the drive.

'It's all right. I'm going home by bus, thanks.' Rosie broke into a trot. The bus conductor was looking at his watch and keeping an eye on the pair of them, in case they should want the bus.

'But I came specially to give you a lift home!' Hal's face, confused and ominously angry, was the last thing she saw before the automatic doors of the bus closed and, revving as if he was in the Grand Prix, the driver pulled away from the stop. Rosie fumbled in her purse for change for the fare, refusing to look over her shoulder and see him again. Her fingers trembled as she counted out the coins and the bus conductor looked at her strangely.

'Bit of problem with your boy-friend?' he enquired as he took the money and punched out a ticket.

'Something like that,' Rosie lied. Hal Dickinson her boy-friend? No, not in a million years. First of all because no one in their right minds would dare call Hal a boy. And secondly because now she understood it all, and it made sense. His kisses, his kindness, were all an act to boost her confidence, increase her loyalty to the place. He had thought that she would blindly trust him, and she had —until those telling words had slipped out from Dr Hillyard's lips. Hal just thought of her as another unfortunate case; he valued her, but he'd also got her summed up as a person with a problem. He had no illusions, obviously. He wasn't in love with her. She stared fixedly out of the window all the way back to Clayburgh and avoided the interested looks of the other passengers.

Rosie plodded through evening surgery feeling empty; empty both of substantial food, because the diet Dr Hillyard had given her to follow didn't seem to involve actually swallowing much at all, and empty of emotion. She tried to think of nothing but the patients. Every time her mind wandered to Hal, to the things he said and the conflicting things he did, she felt confusion beginning to mount inside her. It was almost like being physically sick, this ache of not knowing what to think, and it kept sweeping over her as she coped with the dozen petty and not so petty things that came her way.

The moment the last patient had been seen off, Rosie was galvanised into action, clearing up the surgery. She wanted to get out. She couldn't bear talking to Hal, not tonight—not until she'd had plenty of time to think things over and decided what to do. Her hurt from this afternoon had abated, but remnants of it were still there, as was her confusion about all the things he'd said and done. If only she could trust him. If only she could forget the suspicion which nagged at her that his warmth was motivated by something other than friendship. There were an awful lot of 'if onlys'. Never before, not even in her crush on Dr Levete, had she felt this sense of unease. With him it had been like a dream—not a moment's doubt. But here, faced with something real, something developing . . . She straightened a chair and replaced it in its rightful position. The thing was that with Giles Levete it *had* been just a crush. She'd been too infatuated with him at the time to notice, but he hadn't felt anything for her at all. They'd only been out together once. But with Hal there was an unimagined closeness growing, and because it wasn't just a dream it had all the difficulties and sharp edges of reality. Even so, her memory of this morning's interview with Dr Hillyard was too hurtful to ignore.

Rosie picked up her bag and left the surgery. Once safely inside the flat she put the bolt on the door and went upstairs to make some supper. As she chopped vegetables and checked her diet sheet she heard the banging of the knocker below and, hiding behind the curtain of her sitting-room, she saw Hal peering up at the flat and shaking his head in confusion. Part of her wanted to open the window and shout down to him to wait as he looked up and down the street unsure of where she might be, but she bit back the weakness. She couldn't yet trust him and she didn't understand him. And right at this moment, with Dr Hillyard's scathing words in her ears, she didn't even want to try to trust or understand him.

A giant figure was towering over her, thumping her desk with his hand and making a pounding noise that seemed to rattle and reverberate through her head. 'I'll teach you a thing or two!' his voice boomed, and he was just about to advance on her when the door opened and Hal stood there, white-robed like some sort of knight.

'Don't touch her,' he warned, and his words gladdened Rosie's heart. She ran to him, and he folded her in his arms . . .

Rosie woke up with a start. The pounding noise was for real, not some silly dream, though in a waking instant she recognised Mr Barclay's tall figure and threatening words. Getting out of bed and slipping into the capacious caftan she'd bought off a market stall specialising in Indian goods, she made her way downstairs, switching on the light and taking care not to trip. Her hair, loose for the night, fluffed around her face.

The hammering continued until she opened the door; she wasn't at all afraid of who she'd find —indeed, part of her wanted to discover Hal there. But it wasn't him. Instead it was Mrs Perrin, who served in Clayburgh's bakery and who had been generous in the past with doughnuts and cream cakes.

'Thank goodness, Nurse, you must come quickly. I think my husband's dying!' She tugged wildly at Rosie's sleeve, and in the light from the hall Rosie could see that she was really in a panic.

'Have you called out Dr Higgins?' she asked. 'He's on duty tonight.'

'I've tried to, but I've rung and rung and rung and he's not there. Please Nurse, I'm not having you on,' the anguished woman protested.

'Of course I'll come, but we must call out a doctor—I can't do much for your husband. I'll call Dr Dickinson now and then come with you.' Rosie tried to stay calm. It was easy in such circumstances to allow a patient's over-reaction to panic nursing staff into a state of nerves. Fortunately she'd served her time in Casualty at Highstead and was used to emergencies.

'I've tried it. He's got his answering machine on—he's out on a call at Buckstead. I wouldn't have got you up otherwise, Nurse.' Mrs Perrin looked apologetic but firm. 'George is in such terrible pain, and his breathing's bad. I wouldn't ask you, but I don't know what to do.'

'Give me two minutes. I'll just go and put something on.' Rosie raced upstairs and threw on some clothes. Philip Higgins should be on call tonight, she knew—so why was Hal out? And what was she going to do for Mr Perrin?

Before setting off up the road, she let herself into the surgery while Mrs Perrin stood outside wringing her hands in despair and uttering little murmurs of worry at the delay. Rosie didn't like having to keep the poor woman waiting, but if it was a false alarm then a minute or two wouldn't matter, and if it was serious then she would be better to come prepared. She had her own bag with stethoscope, sphygmomanometer and other bits and pieces which she used for the occasional home visit, and this she collected. She also activated Hal's bleeper, hoping that wherever he was he would return to the surgery once it had gone off. For good measure she also called his home phone number and left a message there on his answering machine. Then, pausing only to stick a note on the clinic door to inform him where they had gone, she went to join Mrs Perrin.

'What's that for?' the woman asked, watching Rosie tape the hastily-scrawled note to the glass.

'I'm hoping that Dr Dickinson will call here on the way back from his visit and that he'll see this,' Rosie explained. It seemed a silly idea, but she hadn't any better ones.

They ran up the road and down the High Street, turning right into the row of cottages where the Perrins lived. As they climbed the stairs Rosie was surprised to see, from the grandmother clock on the landing, that it was only just after midnight. She must have been soundly asleep, for it felt to her as if it really was the middle of the night.

Mr Perrin lay in the middle of the bed. His breathing was fast and shallow and Rosie noticed how pale and clammy his skin was. She filed the signs and symptoms away in her mind. Already the list of things he might be suffering from was beginning to establish itself.

'Do you have any pain?' she asked automatically, approaching him and putting the bag down at the side of the bed.

'I've got a pain in my shoulders,' he volunteered. 'I think I must have done something this evening after Rugby. Me and some of the boys had a bit of a scuffle in the bar. Aaagh!' he moaned as she tried to raise him gently into a sitting position. Rosie took the hint and left him lying flat.

'When he first started to sweat I thought he'd got a touch of flu coming on, but surely it shouldn't hurt like this?' Mrs Perrin chipped in.

'It could be you've damaged your shoulder and this is a shock reaction,' Rosie wondered aloud. 'But something's not right.'

'I've hurt myself before, but nothing like this,' George Perrin agreed.

'You say that you had a scuffle,' Rosie questioned. 'Were you hit in the stomach or ribs? And when did it happen?' As she spoke, she lifted his wrist and began to take his pulse.

'Ten o'clock—a bit later, maybe. Some of us were just mucking about and things got a bit out of hand. I did take a punch in the stomach, but it's not my stomach that's hurting, Nurse.' He looked up at her as if she was mad. Mrs Perrin looked less than impressed too.

Rosie put down the man's wrist and made a note of his pulse rate. It was racing, another bad sign. She ran her hand over his brow. He was cool and clammy. 'Do you normally have a good colour?' she asked casually.

'I've never seen him look so pale!' Mrs Perrin commented. 'That's why I was so worried.'

They were both slightly bemused when Rosie insisted on examining Mr Perrin's abdomen, but complied with her nevertheless. There was no bruising to indicate where he had been hit, and when she very gently palpated his abdomen her patient didn't show much sign of discomfort. Yet

Rosie thought she could feel some rigidity—a slight resistance to her touch. It was impossible to be quite sure, of course, but her instincts told her that the blow to Mr Perrin's abdomen had ruptured something internally. The shoulder pain indicated that it might be the liver or even the spleen. And yet it was impossible to be certain; it might just be acute pain from an injured shoulder. A month ago she wouldn't have hesitated to call an ambulance, but now she did. What if her patient had just pulled a muscle and was really only in need of painkillers? What would Hal and Philip Higgins have to say to that? He had no definite abdominal pain and she could feel no certain evidence of blood in the peritoneal cavity.

She bent again and tapped her fingers lightly over the pale extent of George Perrin's belly. There was some resonance—and there wouldn't be if the area was dulled with blood. Even so, she didn't like it. As she stood there thinking things over carefully and trying to work out the time limits, the phone rang downstairs and Mrs Perrin trotted off to answer it. If Mr Perrin had suffered the blow at ten to half-past ten, there might be another hour or hour and a half to go before anyone could say for certain what the damage was. Maybe she ought to stay with him and observe any changes. A ruptured spleen was a serious business—and so was whipping someone into hospital under false pretences, particularly if you made a habit of it.

'It's for you. It's Dr Dickinson,' Mrs Perrin called up the stairs, and suddenly weak-kneed with relief, Rosie ran down.

'What's the problem?' Hal asked wearily. 'I've just found your message on the answerphone.' He sounded irritable and immediately Rosie bit back her joy.

'Mr Perrin,' she reported in an efficient voice. 'He was in a scuffle this evening and now he's suffering from shoulder pains, racing pulse and pallor. I've examined him and I can't be sure, but I think he's got some sort of visceral rupture.'

'Is he suffering from abdominal pain?' Hal was all ears, she could tell. He was suddenly attentive, professional.

'Slight discomfort, but all the pain's centred in the shoulder area. I'm worried about his . . .'

'Spleen,' they both said together, and they both paused a second with an acknowledging chuckle.

'Or he might just have injured his shoulder,' Rosie added. 'What shall I do?'

'Call an ambulance,' Hal said without hesitation. 'I'm on my way but it'll take me ten minutes.'

'I think I'll wait until you get here,' Rosie prevaricated. 'I don't think that there's any immediate danger and I don't want to get them out on a wild goose-chase——'

'Phone them now, Rosie,' Hal ordered. 'I trust your diagnosis. If you think he's ruptured his spleen, I expect he has. Tell the hospital that I asked you to call an ambulance if necessary, but call one now. The sooner he's surgically investigated, the better.'

'But——' Rosie ventured.

'No buts,' he snapped. 'Do it.' There was a click and then the *brrrr* of the empty line. Rosie put down the receiver, glanced swiftly at Mrs Perrin, and then dialled.

It was a good job she had, too, she decided five

minutes later, for George Perrin's pulse was whirl-
ing away and a new examination of the abdominal
wall revealed increased tenderness and a definite
doughy resistance to her hand. Mrs Perrin, initially
dumbstruck at the emergency call, bustled about
finding clean pyjamas and other bits and pieces for
her husband.

'He will be all right, won't he, Nurse?' she asked
worriedly from time to time as her husband's occasional groans of discomfort grew louder.

Rosie just nodded encouragingly and tried to
calm her. A ruptured spleen could be dangerous,
but they seemed to have caught the trouble in good
time. She helped make Mr Perrin as comfortable as
possible for his journey, helping him into his dressing gown and explaining to him what had happened.

'Has he got time for a cup of coffee or a stiff drink
before he goes?' Mrs Perrin asked anxiously.

'No!' Rosie looked shocked. 'He must have nothing at all to eat or drink if he's to go into Theatre.
They'd have to stomach-pump him otherwise.'

Mr Perrin twitched on the bed and muttered a
strangled, 'Oh God!'

Hal must have driven through the dark lanes at a
phenomenal speed, Rosie thought, to get there in
the time he did. As it was, the screech of his tyres as
he pulled up just past the house alerted them to his
presence. He was wearing jeans and a big sweater;
not, perhaps, the clothes in which a doctor normally goes on visits but as like as not the first things
to come to hand when he'd been woken for the
Buckstead call, Rosie thought. She felt overjoyed
to see him, though she tried hard to hide the
reaction. He greeted her briefly but all attention

was focused on poor Mr Perrin, who submitted himself to one final undignified examination.

'It's a good job you decided to get one of us out,' Hal said sombrely as he straightened up. 'You *did* call the ambulance?' This was directed straight at Rosie, who flushed.

'Of course I did,' she snapped.

'They're getting a bit suspicious of Nurse Simpson,' Hal joked to the surprised Perrins. 'She keeps phoning up and asking for ambulances, you see. Anyone would think that she's the only medic in the area.'

'She's been very helpful, I'm sure,' Mrs Perrin said, nervously stroking her husband's hand as he lay, pale and sweating, in his bed. 'I couldn't get hold of Dr Higgins and I didn't know *what* to do.'

'I'm afraid that Dr Higgins is very elusive at the moment.' Hal's grim smile said far more than his words. They sat in silence for a few moments, waiting and listening. Eventually Hal decided that the ambulance couldn't take much longer and he and Rosie supported Mr Perrin and took him downstairs. Sure enough, within a few minutes the ambulance crew were knocking at the door and the patient had been loaded on to a trolley and placed inside. Mrs Perrin, clutching a carrier bag full of socks and pyjamas and paperback books, climbed in to sit next to the ambulanceman.

'I'll come with you,' Rosie volunteered, suddenly nervous at the thought of being left alone with Hal after all that had happened in the past twenty-four hours. It seemed like a dream now, that visit to the hospital, her rudeness to him, even the scene with Mr Barclay . . .

'No,' he said firmly, and his hand on her arm

checked her. The doors of the ambulance slammed and echoed in the night, and lights went on in windows nearby. In one of them a sash went up and a rumpled head peered out.

'We're going.' Hal's fingers bit into Rosie's flesh as he shut the front door of the house and led her to the car. Without a word he unlocked the passenger door and motioned her to get in. To protest that it was only three hundred yards back to the clinic would have been useless, Rosie knew. And anyway, she had a feeling that something important was about to happen to her. She'd put it off and put it off, but it couldn't be avoided for ever.

It was nice to be driven by Hal; sheer pleasure to have his attention. To be quietly by his side, trusted and relied on, was all she really wanted for the rest of her life.

He parked outside the clinic and when he got out of the car, spotted the note on the door. 'Ingenious,' he laughed, reading it. 'My bleeper went off but when I called in there was no one here, so I thought it must have been malfunctioning.'

'I didn't know how to contact you, so I thought I'd try every possibility,' Rosie explained. 'Do you want to come up for a cup of coffee?' she offered, suddenly shy.

'I have every intention of coming up, whether you want me to or not,' was the cryptic reply, but his eyes were dark and smiling and he sat quietly on a worktop in the kitchen while she made coffee. Every time she passed him to get mugs or spoons or to switch off the kettle he reached out and stroked her hair, teasing and taunting her but never getting too close.

'Why were you so angry with me this morning?'

he asked quietly as they waited for the coffee to drip through the filter into the pot. 'I had some good news for you.'

'Oh!' Rosie tried to inject a note of scorn into her voice, but it was a task beyond her.

'Oh yes—*really*,' he taunted, leaning forward to brush a strand of hair from her cheek. She pushed his hand away in the pretence of annoyance, but he just grinned back at her, swinging his legs. He was so confident, so sure of himself, she thought, and she loved him for it. 'I'd been in to see Mrs Guthrie shortly before I met you.'

'And?' His pause and his unfuriating grin gave nothing away and she was suddenly anxious.

'You were right about her mother—just as you were right about George Perrin. Congratulations. Philip had been informed, as Mrs Norris' GP, that she *was* suffering from Huntington's. However, he decided not to tell us.' Hal was serious again. 'I've had words with him.' His navy eyes glinted with intensity and his fingers gripped the edge of the work surface. 'Now tell me why *you* were so upset. What did Hillyard have to say?'

Rosie shrugged, but he took her by the shoulders and held her in front of him, and she wondered for a moment if he'd shake her if she didn't comply. 'Are there any problems? Tell me!'

'No, there aren't any problems. I've just been put on a no-sugar diet. So you don't have to worry that I'm going to have to interrupt your precious clinic routine for insulin injections or have hypos all over the place,' Rosie said sharply.

'That's the last thing on my mind. Honestly, Rosie, you think I'm a real tyrant, don't you? Do you seriously think that I care more about this place than I do about your health?'

She couldn't help but reply, 'All I know is that you seem to have me—and everyone else too, I expect—in neat little categories.'

'And just what is that supposed to mean?' Hal slid off the worktop and in the confined space of the kitchen his thighs brushed her. She felt trapped at such close quarters with him, and yet she had no thoughts of moving away.

'Well, you've got Philip down as unreliable——'

'With just cause, I hope you'll agree,' he snorted. 'And what have I got you down as?' His hand resting gently on the top of her arm, his concerned glance, the sudden intentness between them, all made Rosie want to drop the subject, to respond positively to him. But she owed it to herself not to duck out, she knew.

'A compulsive eater.'

'Is that what Hillyard told you?' Hal's eyes were dark and deep, not as glittering as they usually were; not full of amusement and quick wit as they usually, were. There was something pained in them.

'And so you were terribly offended—even though it might be true and even though I wrote it out of concern for you?' His voice was low and throaty.

'You see, you don't deny it. Just for the record, I don't happen to agree with your diagnosis and I don't think I need psychiatric help.' Her head swam simply from the effects of his look. Tonight she didn't feel fat and frumpy in his presence. Strangely, she felt in control of things—in control of her life even, which she hadn't felt for a long time. She'd been right about George Perrin and right about Mrs Guthrie; she had no need to doubt her professional competence. And it was odd, but knowing that she really *had* to look after herself if she wasn't to go badly downhill as a diabetic also gave her a feeling of being in control.

'Is that what Hillyard said? He must need it himself! I didn't suggest it, believe me.' And Rosie did. 'But now I need to talk to you about another problem, one that's going to be more difficult to solve.' Hal let go of her shoulder and leaned back against the kitchen cabinet. 'Philip isn't on call tonight because he's handed in his notice and left us. He was embarrassed when I found out about Mrs Norris, of course, but that wasn't his main reason. He's not been very happy here for some time, and his way of doing things isn't necessarily mine.'

'Like using a deputising service instead of doing his own calls,' Rosie commented with a raised eyebrow.

'That, among other things,' Hal agreed wryly. 'Anyway, things came to a head tonight and he decided that the best thing to do was leave right now.'

'The best thing for *him*. Meanwhile his patients . . .'

'Shhh! We've coped. *You've* coped, I should say. I don't want to start recriminations now. After all, I should have been more careful when I selected him for the post.' Hal's finger, which he'd pressed gently to her lips to silence her, now raised her chin so that Rosie had to look him in the eye. 'My main worry is that I'm going to lose my other, more valued, staff.' There was a glimmer in his eye and Rosie suspected that he was half-teasing her.

'Like Mrs Hammond,' she suggested thoughtfully.

'Like Mrs Hammond,' he agreed. 'I think that I have a solution for one case—though unfortunately it won't work with Mrs Hammond.' He frowned, but not so convincingly that Rosie didn't suspect his motives.

'Why wouldn't it work with Mrs Hammond?' she asked, waiting for some jokey reply.

'Because she's already married—to Mr Hammond.' There was a long pause, punctuated only by the drip of coffee into the pot. Rosie looked at the kitchen floor as if she was searching for a contact lens. Her throat felt suddenly dry as she pondered his words—and yet she couldn't trust what she thought he was trying to say in his oblique manner.

'Actually, it wasn't Mrs Hammond I was worried about. It was you. I had a horrible feeling this afternoon when you got on to that bus that you might be planning to do a Philip, and I couldn't stand for that.'

Firm hands gripped her shoulders; she could feel the warmth of his body against hers. 'Marry me, Rosie. Do you think you could bear to do that?'

'Don't be silly.' She pulled back, away from him, her eyes smarting with tears. 'It's quite all right, Hal, there's no need to do anything quite so drastic. I'm not thinking of leaving, though I might if you keep playing these stupid games with me.' She turned away, aware of her scarlet cheeks and a sudden desire to sniff loudly.

'I've done it again!' Hal's words reached her as she walked unsteadily into the sitting-room—unsteadily because the floor seemed to lurch with every step. 'Rosie,' he was suddenly behind her again, 'it wasn't the most elegant of proposals, but I mean it. When will you learn to believe that what I tell you is true?' He swung her round to face him and almost shook her by the shoulders. 'Why won't you trust me? For heaven's sake, I love you, I don't want to hurt you—but you seem determined to turn everything I do or say into some grave insult!'

'I've trusted people in the past,' Rosie heard herself saying, almost in a dream, 'and it's usually gone wrong. There really isn't any need to propose, Hal. I'm not going to leave.' The tears began to run down her cheeks and he wiped them away with his fingers.

'Why won't you even think about it?' he asked quietly. 'Is there someone else?'

'Don't be silly.' Rosie gave a snuffling laugh.

'You don't feel anything for me, then? Be truthful now.' There was that old glittering twinkle in his eye when, with a rueful smile, she glanced up.

'I wouldn't say that,' she admitted.

'You made a youthful vow never to marry, then?' he suggested. 'Or maybe there's something awful in your past that I don't know about?'

'Nothing like that. It's just . . . I'm not the right kind of person for you, Hal. You need someone like Claire—well,' she silenced his protest, 'maybe not exactly like Claire. But not me.'

'I'm being serious now, Rosie. No joking, this is important. I don't know why you do yourself down all the time, though I'm going to make it my job to find out and change it. But I *do* know for sure that you're the woman I want to marry. And I know without any doubt that you're just right for me and this place. From the day you arrived here I've heard nothing but praise and warmth for you—and yet you yourself don't seem to have noticed how much people appreciate you, and love you. It's very stuck-up of you not to acknowledge how much you're wanted and needed here you know. You scurry off at times as if you were frightened . . .'

'In a way I am!' she interrupted. 'Everybody's been so nice, and yet I sometimes feel as if it's all so temporary, as if it's some dream that'll fade——'

'There's one sure way of making certain that it doesn't.' Hal bent his head and kissed her gently on the lips. 'Say you'll marry me. Let me look after you—prove to you that everything good doesn't disappear on the stroke of midnight. You're too good to spend your days hurrying around corners and hiding up here.'

'And what if the diabetes gets worse? Hal, I don't jog, I don't sail—I don't do the things you do!'

'That's part of the plan too. Because I can keep a check on your health. It's going to be tough, I warn you, Nurse Simpson—but there will be some rewards, I promise.' He bent and kissed her again, this time more firmly, and Rosie felt herself responding with a surge of desire and unbearable love that she hadn't known she was capable of. 'Trust me,' he murmured into her hair. 'I'm not trying to change the way you are, but I want the best for you. I love you, Rosie. I never thought I'd hear myself say it, but I do.'

'And you're not just saying it because you want a nurse?' Rosie asked, still unable to believe that it wasn't some elaborate joke.

'Grrrrr! Haven't I *told* you? This is your last chance, you know. You can't expect people to keep on giving you their care and concern if all you do is throw it back at them.' He took her face between his hands and said very slowly, 'Will you marry me?'

Rosie studied those navy eyes, confident, amused and full of something that she could at last put a name to. Marriage to Hal would be a challenge; she didn't think for a moment that it would be all bliss . . . But how could she say no?

'Yes—if you're sure you want to,' she murmured.

'Of course I want to!' Hal stepped back, almost in surprise. 'You said yes. You mean it?' Suddenly it was he who looked questioning, doubtful.

'Oh yes, I mean it!' Rosie agreed. 'What will Mrs Hammond say?'

'Mrs Hammond will simply say that it took us a long time to get round to it,' Hal grinned. 'Two days after you arrived she came clucking in to me to tell me what a paragon you were—and how much better in every way than Claire. And since then she hasn't let up. She'll be relieved that she can stop the campaign. And I tell you, Rosie, if there's anyone who knows what's good for us it's Mrs Hammond.'

'Oh yes. I trust Mrs Hammond,' was all Rosie could say contentedly before she was silenced once more.

 **Mills & Boon**

YOU'RE INVITED TO ACCEPT
4 DOCTOR NURSE
ROMANCES
AND A TOTE BAG

FREE!

Doctor Nurse

Acceptance card

| NO STAMP NEEDED | **Post to: Reader Service, FREEPOST, P.O. Box 236, Croydon, Surrey. CR9 9EL** |

Please note readers in Southern Africa write to:
Independant Book Services P.T.Y., Postbag X3010, Randburg 2125, S. Africa

YES! Please send me 4 free Doctor Nurse Romances
and my free tote bag – and reserve a Reader
Service Subscription for me. If I decide to subscribe I shall
receive 6 new Doctor Nurse Romances every other month as
soon as they come off the presses for £6.60 together with a
FREE newsletter including information on top authors and
special offers, exclusively for Reader Service subscribers.
There are no postage and packing charges, and I understand I
may cancel or suspend my subscription at any time. If I decide
not to subscribe I shall write to you within 10 days. Even if I
decide not to subscribe the 4 free novels and the tote bag are
mine to keep forever. I am over 18 years of age   EP23D

NAME _____
                                              (CAPITALS PLEASE)

ADDRESS _____

_____

_____ **POSTCODE** _____

*Mills & Boon Ltd. reserve the right to exercise discretion in
granting membership. You may be mailed with other offers as a
result of this application. Offer expires March 31st 1987 and is
limited to one per household.*
Offer applies in UK and Eire Only. Overseas send for details.

Loving

Little Heather Fraser had everything she could possibly want, except the love of her father, Jay.

His callousness shocked the tiny Cotswold village, and most of all Claire Richards, whose daughter Lucy was Heather's friend.

When Jay accused Claire of encouraging the girls' friendship so that she could see more of *him*, nothing could have been further from the truth.

A freak accident suddenly put paid to Claire's cherished independence. Would she be able to swallow her angry pride and reluctantly share the Frasers' roof?

After 25 million sales worldwide, best-selling author Penny Jordan presents her 50th Mills & Boon romance for you to enjoy.

Available January 1987
Price £1.50.

Mills & Boon